**Wordsmith**

TELLING TALES

# TELLING TALES – WOW Anthology

Published in 2015 by FeedARead.com Publishing

A CIP catalogue record for this title is available from the British Library.

# Contents

# *Contents*

# Contents

# Foreword

It gives me enormous pleasure to present the first anthology of poetry and prose from the Wordsmiths of Weston. Here is writing at its most creative, a satisfying mix of styles and genres.

A good anthology should contain humour, pathos, tragedy and hope. *Telling Tales* meets all of the criteria with a touch of magic thrown in. Contained within these pages are tales of love lost and found, inspirational gifts, wooden legs and old ladies on a train, a mysterious stone angel and a sartorial giant anteater. We are transported to the wonderfully named Little-Mousing-in-the-Marsh, meet George intent on slaying a dragon in Yatton, and bear witness to an act of kindness from the great El Cid.

This and so much more awaits you in this labour of love from nine talented local authors.

Two of my passions in life are reading and chocolate, and I can liken this collection to a box of luxury Belgian chocolates; once you start on them, you won't be satisfied until you reach the end. And then you will want more.

It is always a joy to read the work of fellow writers, and to see that work in print affords them a kind of immortality.

Alyson Heap
Organiser of the Somerset Short Story Competition
March 2015

*Placed THIRD in the 2012*
*Somerset Short Story Competition*

# Mustn't Grumble

## BRIAN HUMPHREYS

Eight chimes from the old clock downstairs took Jack back to happier times, playing with his Meccano on a threadbare carpet before his late mother, but they had the opposite effect on his wife. 'Do we have to wake up to that racket every morning?'

'What racket?' said Jack, his Meccano spanner slipping from his grasp.

'Your mother's clock.' Lisa eased her aching body out of bed and ripped open the bedroom curtains. 'Looks like rain, and that's no good for my joints, no good at all.'

'Exercise is good for joints. Why don't you go for a long walk?' (*Off a short pier,* he said quietly to himself.)

'You'd like that, wouldn't you?'

Jack imagined her body falling into the sea, the loud splash, and the calm that would follow. 'Yes, my angel.'

'I'm NOT your angel.'

'You left the toilet seat up, again,' moaned Lisa as she followed him downstairs. The clock chimed eight-thirty and Jack smiled, remembering the Christmas morning his mother gave him a shiny red bicycle.

'How many sweeteners do you want, my angel?' he shouted from the kitchen.

'Two. How many times do I have to tell you? I'm NOT your angel!' Lisa banged on the lounge window and the cat on the lawn took flight.

'If next-door's flea-bitten moggie messes on my lawn once more, I won't be responsible.'

'Of course you won't, my angel. The cat will be responsible.'

'I'm NOT your angel, and you know where you can stick your sarcasm.'

During breakfast, Lisa moaned about the weather, her joints, the clock, the government, next-door's cat, and anything else she could think of, whilst Jack, following his late mother's mantra: *don't speak with your mouth full*, finished first, showing his appreciation with a loud belch.

'Do you mind? I'm still eating.'

'Only because you talk so much, Jesus wept!'

'He would've wept, if one of the wise men had given him a clock that chimed every half-hour.'

As if in protest, the clock chimed nine times, and Jack remembered the proud look on his mother's face when he had bought it with his first wage packet, to replace her old cuckoo clock that he had decapitated with his Frisbee. Jack lovingly polished the clock and wound it carefully, two turns of the key, just like Mother used to do until cancer took her from him.

Jack headed for the sanctuary of the back garden; a dull ache was taking hold of his temple and his mouth was turning dry. As he inhaled his first smoke of the day, Lisa's loud voice shattered the silence. 'Were you born in a barn?'

'I think you'll find that was Jesus, my angel,' he fired back.

'I'm NOT your angel. Shut that door; you know draughts play havoc with my joints.'

The telephone rang in the lounge, causing a temporary ceasefire. Despite aching joints, Lisa reached it first. 'Beryl, how are you? I hope this weather isn't getting you down. What? Me? I'm fine, mustn't grumble.'

'Mustn't grumble?' Jack shouted down the hall. 'Mustn't grumble?'

Lisa finished her conversation and found Jack in the kitchen. 'What did you say?'

'I was merely pointing out, my angel...'

'I'm NOT your angel.'

'...that you couldn't go five minutes without a grumble.' The clock chimed once, and Jack remembered his mother's winning bet on the Grand National. 'I bet you £5 you can't go five hours without moaning.'

'Five hours?' The force of her breath pinned his ears to the sides of his head. 'It was five minutes just now.'

'There you go, what did I tell you? You couldn't even last five seconds.'

'Five minutes? Five hours? Five seconds? Make your bloody mind up.'

'Five hours. £5 says you couldn't last five hours without moaning.'

Each chime of that clock reminded Lisa of Jack's mother, the interfering old hag, and she sensed an opportunity to get shut of the clock, once and for all. 'How's this for a bet: if I moan within five hours, you keep the clock, but if I don't, you get rid of it?'

Without hesitation, Jack grabbed Lisa's hand. 'Agreed.' Getting her to moan would be easy; he knew all of her trigger points. He headed for the kitchen to make the tea. 'Is it two sweeteners, my angel?'

Lisa clenched her teeth. 'You'll have to do better than that.'

'Was that a moan?'

'No, dear, just stating facts.'

The clock struck ten, and Jack remembered the proud look on his mother's face the day he passed his driving test. He had failed his mother many times when she was alive; he would not fail her now.

Even towards the end, through the rigours of chemotherapy, she always put on a brave face, never once complaining, unlike his wife, moaner Lisa. He picked up the newspaper. 'I see inflation's up; this coalition government's useless.'

Lisa ground her teeth. 'I'm sure they're doing the best they can.'

The clock struck ten-thirty, and Jack remembered his mother's words at his engagement, '*You deserve better.*'

'Jack, will you give me a hand with the weekly shop?'

'Of course, my angel.'

'I'm NOT...' Lisa caught herself just in time. '...in a hurry; whenever you're ready will be fine.'

Jack was ready in minutes; car journeys and supermarket visits were moaning hotspots. He drove faster than Lewis Hamilton, often cornering on two wheels, but Lisa held on with white knuckles and gritted teeth. Inside the supermarket, Jack dawdled, even accidentally ran the trolley into the back of her legs, but Lisa, even though she was madder than a bipolar bear with toothache, stayed silent. They returned home, the clock struck twelve-thirty, and Jack remembered the reading of his mother's will and the return of his clock with a note: 'In memory of happy times.'

'Let's synchronise our watches, Jack. I make the time just turned twelve-thirty.'

Jack checked his watch, and the clock on the mantelpiece. 'Agreed.'

Lisa rubbed her hands together. 'Haven't those three hours flown by? Only two hours to go. In place of that clock, I think I'll put a nice plant.'

Jack wanted to plant a right hook on Lisa's chin, but his late mother hated violence.

When the clock struck one, Jack became more and more desperate, the magnitude of the bet weighing heavy on his shoulders. He picked his nose, he passed wind so loudly the windows rattled, but Lisa stayed silent. When the clock struck one-thirty, panic set in. 'If you don't engage in conversation, the bet's off, because that's cheating.'

'The bet did not say speaking was compulsory.'

'Was that a moan?'

'There's only one person moaning, Jack, and it isn't me.'

When the clock struck two, each chime was like a dagger in Jack's heart. He rounded up next-door's cat and threw it on Lisa's lap. She quickly sent the cat flying with a backhand swat that Martina Navratilova would have been proud of. 'One more chime, Jack, and you lose.' There was a defiance in her tone that Jack was determined to squash, somehow.

With minutes left, Jack gave Lisa the garage key. 'Will you fetch a bottle of wine from the garage? At least let me raise a glass to wish the clock farewell; I'm obviously going to lose.'

Lisa jumped to her feet. 'It will be my pleasure.' Minutes later, she returned, bottle of wine in hand.

Jack threw the dice one last time. 'All the times you've asked, "Does my bum look big in this?" Well, it does. It looks big in everything!'

Lisa's blood began to boil; he had gone too far. Her arms turned red, her neck turned blue, her face turned purple, her heart was racing, steam poured from her ears, she panted like a woman in childbirth, snorted like an angry bull, her fists clenching and unclenching, she could hold back no longer. Jack lurched back in self-defence; any second now, she would explode.

The clock struck once, and Lisa erupted. 'Time's up, loser. I win, so take that bloody clock, and shove it where the sun doesn't shine!'

Jack straightened slightly. 'Was that a moan, my angel?'

'You know damn well it was. AND I'M NOT YOUR ANGEL!'

With slumped shoulders, Jack moved towards the mantelpiece. Lisa grinned like a Cheshire cat, until Jack picked up the phone, dialled three numbers, and passed it to her. 'It's for you.'

Why wasn't he upset? She raised the handset to her ear.

'*At the third stroke, the time from BT will be two twenty-nine and ten seconds precisely...*'

Lisa dropped the phone and checked her watch. Two twenty-nine.

'Oh dear,' said Jack, polishing the clock with loving care. 'While you were in the garage, I wound the clock one last time. Silly me, I must have knocked the minute hand, and you've moaned before two-thirty, and that makes me the winner. Never mind, I'll go and put the kettle on. Is it two sweeteners, my angel?'

*Placed THIRD in the 2014*
*Somerset Short Story Competition*

# *The Giant Anteater*

### FAITH MOULIN

"Is a giant anteater called a giant anteater because it's big, or because it eats giant ants?"

It was a sensible question, but the girl's mother laughed. "It's because it's big."

It was on that very same day, a fantastical day in the history of aviation and evolution, that an anteater caught a plane from Rio de Janeiro to London. The air stewardess welcomed him aboard: "Are you travelling alone, sir?"

"Oh yes," the anteater said, "I'm used to taking care of my own needs. I don't need company."

"I won't seat anyone next to you, then," the stewardess said. "Someone might not like your tongue."

The anteater sat alone, silently staring ahead with his small eyes, until she returned with a tray of drinks.

"You're dressed for London, sir, in your beautifully smart clothes," she said. The anteater was pleased, she noticed. He was clad in glorious greyscale like a City man's Savile Row suit; he smoothed his black waistcoat, his white gaiters, his black boots and his long whiskers, bristly as a badger's. His chest hair was closer than a close shave, his tail like a plume of black smoke rising behind him up the back of the seat.

"Yes," said the anteater. "Thank you. They're the cold-climate range from Amazon." He smiled his toothless smile, wrinkling the very tip of his very long nose, and the stewardess smiled back.

"I'll get you a glass of champagne, sir."

The anteater found the champagne flute a very inconvenient shape, but with the help of his pink tongue he was able to sip it, slurp it, spill it and siphon it up. The bubbles went up and up his very long nose; they rose to the top and further. He had never tasted champagne before and it really had gone to his head.

When the plane was standing in the air queuing for runway space at Heathrow, the anteater looked down on all the people, as small as ants, scurrying around, hurrying to land the plane. He said, "I'm going to like it in London. It's full of food. Foreign food, but plenty of it!"

The air stewardess laughed.

The anteater stepped out of the plane into a barrage of flashbulb fire. He blinked. Was there a celebrity on board? The photographers shouted to him, "What do you think of London?" "Give us a sound-bite."

He was feeling very strange. His feet seemed a long way down. Everything was getting smaller and further away; the plane was almost insignificant now, its engines quietly purring like a sleeping jaguar. The journalists and photographers were shouting more and more quietly. He could hardly hear them, they were so far away. They were very small. As small as ants, and his interest in travel and transport began to recede.

*Ants,* he thought. *Ants!* He had outgrown his veneer of civilisation and his aspiration to evolve into a businessman. His animal instincts rose to the surface, to the surface of his tongue. *Yummy. Ants. My favourite.*

The tongue was flicking and licking and the prey was sticking helplessly in the thick saliva. The people didn't know whether to run or to hide, but in the end it didn't matter because the giant anteater's tongue stuck to them and he sucked them all up like tea-leaves up a Dyson Animal.

Eye-witnesses who had escaped were interviewed on the television evening news. The newsreader suggested they had mistaken a jumbo jet or a barrage balloon for a giant anteater. One said, "Where are the two thousand missing people, then?"

When the champagne began to wear off, the giant anteater found his new food was beginning to stick in his throat. He had to spit out suitcases, prams and baggage trolleys. The ground was coming up to meet his nose; even the plane seemed to be getting closer and larger.

"I'm shrinking," he said, the realisation coming slowly like the evening mist over the forest. The plane was getting bigger by the minute. They were about equal size when the anteater realised he was going to end up where he had started. He couldn't possibly vacuum up the people now – they were much too big – but all this shrinking had made him hungry again. There were no ant-hills to be seen at Heathrow.

"I'm not going to fit in here in this grey world of hard landscaping," he said, "even if my clothes do look right." By the time he had finished the sentence he was not such a giant anteater and he was feeling very odd indeed. He was alone in a world of unanswered questions and he was slightly frightened of the people in white coats who were gathering like vultures behind a stripy barrier. One of them had a gun.

"I'm going to try talking to him," said a female white-coat.

"Oh no you're not," said a man resembling a capuchin monkey.

The female ignored her companion and walked towards the anteater. "Can you understand me?" she asked.

"Of course," he said.

"What happened to you?"

"I don't know," he said. "I'm just an anteater, not an analyst. When I saw ants I ate them. That's what I do. That's what all anteaters do. I just can't help myself. It's in my genes."

"Can you promise not to do it again?" the female asked.

"No, of course I can't! Didn't you understand? I'm an anteater. If men look like ants I'm bound to eat them."

"Are you going to grow again into a giant giant anteater?"

"I don't know," the anteater said. He was sad now. He hadn't asked for their champagne, he didn't want their baggage handlers and their passengers and pilots. He only wanted ants. He moved towards the nice female, to reassure her, to talk more intimately so they didn't need to shout. He thought she would like that, but she backed off.

Wrongly interpreting the movement, the marksman lifted his rifle. He couldn't risk another massacre. The animal was unpredictable. It might not even have any control over its size, or its actions.

The girl who had been watching it all on the television in her Hounslow bedroom said, "The anteater's not a giant any more."

Her mother laughed and looked out of the window just as the shot rang out.

# *Spring Nightsounds*

## PETER CORRIN

It's a moonbright garden at frog-croak
And the stars seem to glisten with life,

The clouds have gone to play out of sight
And the air has an edge like a knife.

All colour's distorted by moonlight
To shades of a washed monotone

And the shadows of shadows conceal
The spirits of daylight long flown.

The air quakes with no sound apparent
And excitement seems to shiver abroad

As the night waits for something expected
Like the sound of a withdrawing sword.

And then the night's shattered by noises
As the chorus of frogs' voices soar
And the hidden amphibians
Raucously start their evening's encore.

# The Bucket List

## LYNDA HOTCHKISS

David stared at his reflection and noticed nothing had changed since his diagnosis. He sighed. Why was Fate so unfair? And why did it always happen to him? He was only thirty-six and enjoying life. He had just got engaged to a wonderful girl called Helen, but, two years on, she had found she couldn't cope with his illness and the constant hospital appointments. There had been tears at their parting but he couldn't make her stay; that would be unfair.

Now, three years after he had received the bad news, he knew he was on borrowed time. He had asked not to be told how long he had left, but had spent the last twelve months on his list, a bucket list.

His bucket list was ten items long, and the first three were already ticked. Number four was crossed through. He had had no luck with number five – yet – and number six was outside his grasp completely. He was dealing with number seven tomorrow.

The local news was full of it. A local retired headmaster had been found dead at his home. Early reports said he had been found in his car with the engine on and a pipe from the exhaust running through the driver's window. Charles Dunlop had lived in the village for over fifty years, ever since he was appointed as headteacher at the local school. A harsh disciplinarian, he had ruled it with some severity, but it had brought great results in the standard of education the children in his care had received. Sometimes there had been conflict with pupils – and their parents, even with the governing body, but Charles always claimed to do what he did for the good of the school.

His wife, Beryl, had died in a freak accident while their twin sons were quite young, but Charles had managed to raise them to manhood without help. Only six months ago, the elder (by thirteen minutes) had died in a climbing accident. The rope had given way while he was on holiday in Scotland. Charles had found it more difficult to come to terms with burying his son than to cope after the death of his wife. It was suggested in the media that the death of Hamish, his son, had precipitated his suicide.

David read the front page of the local paper. Mr Dunlop had been headmaster when he had gone to school, and David had often been called to Dunlop's office for attitude and behaviour. There had been a couple of suspensions, several canings and too many detentions to remember. David gave a wry smile. "What goes around comes around, eh, Dunlop?" He started to laugh but his laughter turned to coughing. The paper was dropped to the floor to join several others.

For Inspector Nigel Hawke, the Dunlop case seemed cut and dried. Loss of son coupled with loneliness led to the man taking his own life. Only one thing was out of place in the theory – the wedding invitation on the mantelpiece. In three weeks' time, Charles Dunlop was expected to give a reading at the marriage of his surviving son, Patrick. Hawke somehow felt it was unlikely that a father would kill himself so close to such a happy event.

The hospital appointment passed without David bothering to attend. He didn't want more tests, or to be told that the sands of time were running out. He just wanted to take each day as it came, good or bad.

Inspector Hawke was enjoying a night off. He had a glass of foaming beer in his hand, slippers on his feet and the match was about to start. His wife was busy baking in the kitchen and his kids were out doing what kids do on a Saturday night. This was bliss!

Martin Bradshaw was also watching the match. Wearing his favourite team's colours, he cracked open another can of lager and took a long slug. He coughed slightly and wiped the froth from his upper lip before letting out a long and satisfied "Aaaah!"

Alone in his little flat on the third floor, he reached for the big meat pie he had gone to purchase on the way home. Steak and mushroom – his favourite. He remembered there had been another customer who had actually bought and paid for this very pie, a tall thin bloke with straggly hair and dark-rimmed eyes. Martin had opted for a simple cheese and onion pastie as second-best but had been accosted outside the bakery by the steak-and-mushroom-pie man. There had been the offer of a trade – pie for pastie – if he would like it. Like it? He had lusted for the pie with its rich gravy that ran down your chin with the first bite. He had fantasised about the crisp savoury pastry, the tender and juicy pieces of steak. He couldn't believe his luck, and agreed instantly.

"I really shouldn't eat meat," said the purchaser of this savoury masterpiece as he handed it over to Martin. "It's not good for me, so you are actually saving me from myself by taking it. Tell you what, keep your pastie as well. A bit too rich for me, I think. Enjoy them both."

Now Martin stared at the pie, his mouth salivating in anticipation of the burst of flavours about to assail his taste buds. He licked his lips, then sank his teeth into the golden crust. Two minutes later, he wiped the crumbs from his lap, and reached for the pastie. Not as tasty as the pie, it met the same fate.

Ten minutes later, the home team scored. "Goooooo-alllll!" shouted Martin, punching the air with delight. "You beauties!"

He drank the rest of his lager. He began to sweat and there was a tight feeling in his chest. He was finding it hard to catch his breath.

The crowd went wild as the score went to 2–2.

The phone rang. Hawke reached out for the receiver, never taking his eyes off the screen. His team had just equalised and there were sixteen minutes to go till the final whistle.

"Hawke," he grunted.

It was his sergeant, Howard Pitts. A body had been found on waste ground at the back of the local supermarket. Hawke groaned and pressed the record button.

The body was female, about thirty-five to forty years of age, and fairly well dressed. She was identified as Susan Masters, secretary and mother of three. She had been strangled.

The coroner dealt with the body and Hawke spotted something white on the ground. It was a small round item, probably a tablet. He bagged it and passed it to his sergeant. "Take it to forensics. Might be nothing but we'd better be sure. There's been too many deaths in the last few months and we have so few leads to go on."

The sun was setting when David reached the beach. He had had enough. The pain was more than he could bear, and the little white tablets were not working. He stripped to his blue boxers, tucked his socks into his loafers and placed them on top of the neatly folded pile of clothes. He breathed deeply and relaxed. So this was it!

The water was cold between his toes but he never wavered in his determination. His mind was clear but the pain was overtaking his senses. He walked slowly and steadily, feeling the sand move slightly under his feet. The water was swirling round his waist. A couple of waves were stronger than the rest and they splashed his chest and face. He gasped and stood still for a moment before continuing slowly until the water came up to his neck. He could barely feel his feet now and the cold was permeating his every fibre, numbing some of the pain. Two more paces and the water was under his nose. He could smell its saltiness. He lifted his head and sniffed the air before ducking down. He allowed the water to take him, giving only a brief struggle as it trickled down his nose and filled his lungs. In its darkness, he found his release.

"Not another body!" groaned Hawke. "I've only been in bed two hours!"

His wife mumbled something and turned over, taking the duvet with her. Hawke climbed wearily out of his warm cocoon and got dressed. An hour later he was on the beach looking at the cold body of a man in his mid-thirties.

"No signs of violence," said Pitts.

"So why am I here?" spat his inspector, irritated and tired.

"Thought you might be interested in this," came the cocky reply.

Hawke looked at the smug smile on his sergeant's face, then at the piece of paper inside the plastic evidence bag he was holding.

"A shopping list?" he asked.

"A bucket list," Pitts replied. "But one with a difference." There was that smug smile again.

"Explain."

"A bucket list is a list of things people want to do before they die."

"Don't insult my intelligence," Hawke snarled. "Just get on with it."

"This is a different bucket list. It is a list of names of people."

"So it is a list of names, so what?"

Pitts gave a dramatic little cough for effect before reading the list.

*"Joe Partridge – 12 Denver Place; school bully. Terence Cleaver – flat 5, Temperance Place; beat me to being school captain. Harry Wentworth-Peele – Craven House; stole my first girlfriend. Paul McVay – 15..."*

"Hang on. Those three names. Partridge found dead by the road after a hit-and-run. Cleaver found hanging in the car factory and thought to have been the victim of an accident. Wentworth-Peele – found stabbed in a back alley in the small hours, said to have been the result of a drunken fight."

"Yes, sir, and McVay moved to Ireland after his business collapsed. The next name, Eamonn Pitcher, is untouched, but I did find out that he emigrated to New Zealand about twenty years ago. The next name,

Peter Harrison, died in a gas explosion along with twenty others the year after he left school, but then comes Charles Dunlop – Arden Cottage, Pinner Lane; headmaster from hell."

Hawke started to see things more clearly. "Dunlop. Found in a car and thought to have committed suicide. Monoxide poisoning. Who is this guy?" He pointed at the body on the beach.

Pitts flicked his pocketbook open. "This is David Owen, unemployed gasfitter of 9 Mercury House, Yeovil Gardens. This list was written by him. He was interviewed in connection with the first three names. He was apparently taking a walk when Partridge was killed. In fact, Owen gave a description of the vehicle – which has never been traced. He was apparently an acquaintance of Cleaver, or at least they were both in the same quiz team, being old boys of Dunlop's school. He was in the same club as Wentworth-Peele on the night of his stabbing, but witnesses claimed Owen was paralytic at the time."

Hawke rubbed his chin.

"Next on the list comes Martin Bradshaw, who was found in his home a week ago and thought to have died of a fit. According to Owen's list, Bradshaw got the job Owen had applied for by pretending to be Owen. Thing is that job was with McVay's Buildings, and the firm went bust about six years ago. McVay went back to Cork and has not been heard of since. He was one step ahead of a couple of court warrants and the VAT man. He also abandoned a girl back here. She was expecting his baby and died giving birth. Her name was Alison Owen, David's only sister."

"Is Susan Masters listed?"

"No, but Susan Prentice is. Susan Prentice worked on the counter in the job centre until her marriage six years ago to Colin Masters."

Hawke walked round the body, looking at every bruise and scratch on it. "What's the betting she dealt with Owen after McVay's collapsed?"

Pitts shrugged and nodded in one movement. He made a note in his pocketbook to follow that point up a little more.

"Ten things to do before you die, or in this case, ten acts of revenge. A kick-the-bucket list. Who is the tenth name, Pitts?"

"Nigel Hawke – 312 High Street; copper."

# *Sticky Fingers*

### SALLY ANN NIXON

Wrench in hand, he slipped along the landing, making for the main bedroom at the end of the corridor. The house was cluttered, dusty, dark, silent, and he moved carefully to avoid the piles of newspaper and boxes. He had made no noise forcing up the porch window, sliding his long, skinny frame through the opening. He had watched the house all day. Only an old biddy, scuttling out to the bins and back. No dog, no carer. All on her own. Easy, easy meat.

He froze at the bedroom door, as a small, snicking sound hissed out of the darkness. He waited but still nothing stirred. Taking a breath he went on; there would be some jewellery, cash, his for the taking and the silly old bat wouldn't hear a thing.

He eased open the door and something sweet and sticky touched his face. Reaching up, his hand met thick, gluey thread hanging from the door. Another thread snaked around his ankle, then another. A tug, and he crashed down, hitting his head on the door jamb.

He wriggled, groaned and struggled to focus on the bizarre figure crouched on the bed before him. Scanty hair in curlers, woolly pink bedjacket, slick silky skeins sprouting from her fingertips and mouth, eight eyes glittering evilly.

"Good evening, my dear. Such a long wait for someone so young, so thin, so suitable. No! Don't struggle, don't lose your head. It isn't time yet, then it's mine. Just come into my parlour."

# The Writer

## BARBARA EVANS

Daily I dig deep. I exhume my hidden and buried ideas and I bring them all to the surface and put them on show. I unlock them from their safe-stored verbal vault and drag them into the light.

I pour out mental mixtures of words. I try to tempt and titillate with spicy speech and added appetising prose for others to consume. It takes a long time, for it has to be gently brewed to bring out its full flavour. I give it my full attention. I slowly slide and spill my text out onto the silent space of an empty page. I write.

Phrases, prose and poesy, language and lyric; words sing out in chorus. They leap and lie, they have individual life. They wait to be called or they jump to the front of the queue. They jostle one another, they fight to be first. Every day they clamour to be heard. They surprise; they arrive unannounced. Often I do not see them creep onto the page. Sometimes a single word shows the way, sometimes it is a phrase.

I try them, I test them. I push them like infants towards their first day at school. I place them amongst strangers. They sit alongside unfamiliar companions. I coerce them into ill-fitting places. They are reluctant to go.

I regiment them into obedient lines and review them on parade. They are awkward, they make irregular ranks, for some of them are bigger than others. Some words are audacious, angry or awesome. Some words are soft, sensuous or silver-gilt. Some words are grandiose, or gentle and genuine, and some words are composed of calm and quiet. Many are ordinary rank and file, regular and reliable. They are bare and bountiful, great and gross; they stand beside and against one another.

I assemble them together under a united banner. I check them for smartness. I nudge their disparate shapes into uniform rows. They

26

stand mute in defiles for universal inspection. Everyone must come to see. They must be accessible to all.

My banner should span the world. My colours will be visible for miles. They must cross continents. They are my colours, and my colours are bright.

# Day Trip to Dawlish

### JENNY MURPHY

Never underestimate the scatter-speed of thirty-six oldies with an impressive collection of hurdles to overcome. At least six were partially-sighted, four were diabetic, twelve carried walking sticks or other apparatus, and as for the rest, me included, our defects were not exactly hidden. By the time the train should have arrived, some were in the toilet, others in the lift, while the rest had excelled themselves athletically by tackling the footbridge and were waving from the other side of the track. When the announcement came that the train had been cancelled, all of those feats had to be accomplished in reverse.

Although I hot-footed it to the station master's office, I was beaten to the post by the most vocal member of our party. The fount of all knowledge had already engaged the station master in a complex discussion of possible scenarios rendering him speechless and bewildered. Drastic action was required. I nudged her out of the door and back onto the platform in one swift and only slightly unkind move. Picking up the reins, I explained our predicament in as concise a language as I could manage, trying to gain as much empathy and advantage as possible.

He too was having problems. The next train was not stopping, and the one after was fully booked. His eventual solution was, bless his cotton socks, to supply a bus to take us to Taunton where a more frequent service would progress our journey.

On the platform, little groups were in deep conversation trying to second-guess the outcome of this drama. Two wanted to go home already and one lady was staging a sit-down protest while clutching her shopping trolley. No amount of reasoning was going to change her decision to await a train on her platform. She intended to be in Dawlish and back by 4pm as she had a doctor's appointment. At this rate, she would be fortunate if she got to any destination by 4pm, never mind back. Rumours were rife, and news updates few and far between. Rations of bottled water were distributed freely to the group (much to the annoyance of the fount of all knowledge, who missed the opportunity while in the coffee shop).

The announcement that we were on our way by coach, which was now waiting outside the station for us, was greeted by a mini-burst of energy. I began to herd my stampeding party out of the railway station and towards our bus. A sheep husbandry qualification would have come in very useful. As the coach doors closed, I tried to count the bobbing heads, remembering that we were one down due to the protest strike on the platform. Apparently, she was being looked after by a 'self-confessed' widower when last spotted. In mid-count, I came across the two wildcards of this journey. It transpired that this couple were also heading for Dawlish and had decided to avail themselves of our bus, even stowing their suitcases in the boot for good measure.

The journey to Taunton station was smooth and our travellers were soon chatting happily. We were met with nothing but kindness as we disembarked and explained our difficulty to the first railway employee. He could help us to the next part of our journey but we would have to change trains for one last time. Having negotiated a range of steps and bridges, we were now seasoned travellers equipped to tackle anything. In fact, the next half of our journey was uneventful as we stared out of the train windows and wondered when or if we would see the sea.

As we alighted on the new platform, problem number one was fairly instant. We were standing next to the Dawlish train but apparently it was overloaded and, for the sake of safety, no more passengers would be allowed on board. I scanned the noticeboard and soon discovered that a forty-minute wait was inevitable. Using my now finely-honed herding skills, we settled into a handy waiting room while I tried to impart a message of jolly adventure to the jaded bunch.

Finally, what should be our train pulled in. A battle commenced as the hungry, tired oldies fought determinedly for a seat. Out of nowhere came Attila the Hun in the guise of a female train manager. She asked to see our tickets and then screamed, 'Get them off,' the 'them' being some of my group who had squeezed aboard the train. This task would prove impossible, so I didn't even make an attempt to comply.

'Get them off my train!' Attila the Hun shouted again. 'I'm not delaying my train for you lot.'

No amount of reasoning, begging, pleading or arguing was going to make her change her mind. Suddenly, she stopped shouting, blew her whistle and jumped aboard, slamming the door behind her. The train chugged away with half of my group, leaving a set of open-mouthed onlookers including yours truly.

I flew up the station steps, over the bridge and into the station master's office, only to be handed a complaint form and the advice that the next train was also delayed, and would arrive in twenty-nine minutes. Defeated, we shuffled back into the holding pen.

The remainder of our journey was uneventful and we finally stepped off the train into the seaside metropolis of Dawlish. The first sight to greet us was our missing companion, complete with the attentive widower. 'Great to see you,' she said. 'Must dash if I'm going to be back by 4pm.' With that, the pair trotted off, sharing the shopping trolley for support, never to be seen again.

In order to sample the delights of Dawlish, the people who I could actually find decided to delay their return. One of the party told me that she had never had so much fun until she had joined my group. Slightly mellow after plenty of coffee and a portion of fish and chips, I puffed up my chest on receipt of this rare compliment, and as I preened myself, she went on to explain that the main reason she enjoyed my trips had nothing to do with my efficiency or empathy, but rather the fact that, until she came across me, she had never been thrown off a train.

# The Gun Crew

## GUY JENKINSON

"OK, you miserable shower!" barked the Sergeant. "I'm the Gun Captain of this piece and I require a good crew for it – however, I suppose you lot will have to do."

The four of us stood stiffly to attention in front of a 40mm Bofors anti-aircraft cannon. The Sergeant looked us up and down. A tall, lean man with a fearsome moustache, he'd seen action in France, North Africa and Italy... now he was about to mould four very raw recruits into an efficient gun crew.

He pretended to strike his brow in mock grief. "What *did* I do in a past life to deserve this?" he asked, turning his eyes heavenward, before continuing, "Well, you may have broken your mothers' hearts... but you won't break mine!"

For centuries, some form of those venerable words had been snarled by grizzled NCOs struggling to turn youngsters into soldiers, from Roman decurions shouting in Latin through generations of the world's armies and on into the present day.

Overcoming his feigned despair, the Sergeant addressed us briskly. "From the left you are, respectively: Trainer, Pointer, Loader One, Loader Two – clear?"

In unison, we shouted, "Yes, Sarge!" as we'd been taught to do in basic training.

"OK. At ease... stand easy; gather round." We relaxed from attention as the Sergeant addressed us. "Now I'll show you how it all works."

He pointed to me. "You, Trainer, get up there onto the mount and park yourself in that small metal seat on the right-hand side of the barrel, then" – he gestured to the next in line – "you, Pointer, sit in the one on the left side... and don't touch anything yet!"

As we scrambled to our designated positions, the Sergeant ordered the loaders to stand on either side of the breech mechanism whilst he took his place at the rear of the mount, next to the ammunition racks.

"Right, men, this is simplicity itself. Trainer, you control the gun's traverse; as you wind that hand-crank in front of you the barrel moves left or right – all *you* have to do is keep the target in your sights, in the horizontal plane... OK?"

"Understood, Sarge!" *Sounds easy enough*, I thought, *but it's going to be difficult to see the traverse-sight past the front splinter-shield.* Our instructor seemed oblivious to my lack of height as he turned to my fellow crewman, ensconced in the left-hand seat.

"Pointer, you control the gun's elevation; you wind your crank to move the barrel up or down, whilst all the time you must keep the target in your sights in the vertical plane... understood?"

"Yes, Sarge!"

*Well, Pointer's taller than me, so elevation's probably going to be OK.*

Lastly, the two loaders were given equally brief instruction in how to take clips from the ammunition racks and drop them into the breech shell-feed mechanism.

The Sergeant beamed affably. "There we are; it's so simple a child could do it! Now let's see if you lot can all work together as a gun crew.

"Loader Two," he barked, "pass two clips from the ammunition rack to Loader One, then you must keep him supplied for as long as we're firing. You'll have to work hard; those clips weigh thirty-five pounds each."

Addressing the left-side loader, he said, "This gun fires one hundred and twenty two-pound shells per minute; your job is to feed it a clip every couple of seconds!"

As the first four-round clip passed between the loaders, the Sergeant continued, "The loading slide holds two clips, so you put in the first one, then the second and push down so the first round is rammed... then we're ready to commence firing."

These clips being loaded, the Sergeant placed his foot next to the firing pedal and shouted, to no one in particular, "Gun crew ready for orders!" as he scanned the horizon, shading his eyes with his hand. After a pause, he barked, "Aircraft bearing oh-four-five degrees, height five hundred feet, range three thousand yards – engage target – rapid fire... fire at will!"

Whirling the hand-crank frantically, I traversed the gun to the right; out of the corner of my eye, I saw Pointer's hands in a blur of motion, elevating the barrel to the required angle. The Sergeant – as the Gun Captain – pressed the firing pedal...

BANG! BANG! BANG! BANG!

*"Clip!"*

BANG! BANG! BANG! BANG!

"Cease fire! Target destroyed – well done!"

We relaxed at our posts, feeling great satisfaction that the exercise had concluded so well, and the Sergeant seemed to agree with us: "Well done, men – not bad for novices – although a *really* well-trained crew can sustain that rate of fire for a six-clip burst: twenty-four shells. Anyway, that completes your Bofors training."

He smiled. "OK, stand down, gun crew: dismissed! Go to the cookhouse and get something to eat."

So we did, leaving the Main Ordnance Building with its fascinating contents, to make our way to the Depot Manager's bungalow where my aunt would provide us four with tea and biscuits, for which 'the Sergeant', my uncle, would join us.

The year was 1955 and I was ten years old; I was 'Trainer' and my eight-year-old brother was 'Loader One'. My cousins, aged eleven and twelve, were the other two crew members: 'Pointer' and 'Loader Two'.

My ex-army uncle, a civil servant in charge of a Ministry of Defence ordnance depot, allowed us to play in and around his domain – and what a playground that was!

Whilst my uncle had indulged our imagination as captain of the 'gun crew', he had indeed trained us to man an actual, working Bofors gun, although the 40mm shells that we'd handled were inert dummies; after all, we four could (and did!) get into quite enough trouble with Bonfire Night fireworks. That is, however, another story entirely...

Mind you, I wonder what the British army of the time would have made of a girl loader?

# *Dead Wood*

## VICTORIA HELEN TURNER

It was a still summer Sunday, somewhere in England. The champagne had just been put on ice, when Adelaide sighed. Was it only three months ago that *he* had raised his glass of champagne to her? It seemed more like a hundred years. She'd been wearing one of her new gowns, the latest thing for the spring of 1880. It was her favourite shade of blue. Oh yes, she could still turn a man's head, in spite of what the skirt of her gown concealed!

To strangers, she appeared to walk with a limp. Only she and close friends knew that her skirt concealed a wooden leg which began just below the knee. It was the legacy of a failed elopement in her youth, when, with Papa in pursuit, her galloping horse, following that of her lover, had slipped in the icy road. Adelaide and her horse had fallen, the mare landing on her leg and crushing it. Love affair and leg were amputated, leaving her with a wooden heart to complement her wooden leg, until three months ago when a man with eyes the colour of the sea in stormy weather raised a glass of champagne to her, and smiled at the woman with the blue eyes, blue gown, champagne-coloured hair, and wooden leg – and her wooden heart at last caught fire.

"Who is he?" she asked her hostess.

"John Campbell, a wealthy Scottish architect. A widower twice over, but no children," she was told.

Before the evening was over, Miss Adelaide Wilson, wealthy spinster, was introduced to John Campbell and love at first sight sparkled like champagne.

"Your wives must have died very young, Mr Campbell," she remarked, when he called on her the next day.

"Yes, indeed. They were both young, beautiful, and consumptive."

"How very sad for you, Mr Campbell," murmured Adelaide.

"Indeed yes, my dear Miss Adelaide, but we mustn't live in the past, especially when I see before me a most beautiful present and future."

When he proposed, Adelaide blushed and almost said yes immediately, before she remembered her wooden leg. "There's something you should know, sir," she began.

John Campbell took her hand. "Miss Adelaide, through a mutual friend, I already know about your tragic accident. I wouldn't mind if you had a wooden head; I should love you all the more."

So she said "yes", they became engaged, and in a month they were married and took up residency in John's house, where Adelaide was very happy until the day her husband returned to his business in the town.

There was just one little thing about his house that puzzled her: the cupboard in his study that he always kept locked. Despite her request to see inside, he had refused to open it. In his hurry to leave for work in town, he had left his keys on the desk, and Adelaide could not resist the opportunity.

After trying several keys, she managed to unlock the cupboard. The door creaked slowly open and the blood drained from her face as she laid eyes on the horrifying, obscene contents of the cupboard. Two wooden legs, very like her own, stood inside, labelled 'Mary Anne' and 'Elizabeth'. The cold hand of terror touched Adelaide's newly-awakened heart. Mary Anne and Elizabeth were the names of John's first two wives, and, like herself, they had been wealthy heiresses. She'd heard the rumours that John wasn't as wealthy as was supposed, and that he gambled and was often in debt, and she herself had noticed that he drank to excess. What if he had married them for their money, murdered them, and collected their wooden legs as trophies? She had no doubt that, like her, they must have had wooden legs. Would her leg soon stand in the cupboard, labelled 'Adelaide'?

Her once light-as-champagne heart now sparkled with hatred. She returned the keys to the desk, and shut herself in the cupboard, peeping through the keyhole as the shadows lengthened into darkness.

The front door banged; footsteps came into the study and paused by the desk. "That's where I left my keys," she heard John say.

She took up the wooden leg marked 'Mary Anne' and slowly opened the cupboard door. She crept softly up behind John Campbell, raised the leg, and struck him again and again and again. He slumped into a heap of sticky, bloody blackness, oozing and snaking like Adelaide's hatred until it was lost in the shadows.

"The first two wives died from natural causes," the lawyer told her, "and though, no doubt, their money was useful, he was genuinely fond of them and the wooden legs were kept out of pure sentiment."

It was a still summer day somewhere in England as Adelaide sipped a last glass of champagne, giving, for an instant, a bright sparkle to the grey prison walls. Tomorrow, she would hang.

# *Human*

## BARBARA EVANS

Through the holes that hide me,
Under the arrows that guide me,
I will come and I will go,
I will learn, and will not know.
My own mistakes I will make,
Body blows I will take.
Bleeding, bruised, shamed and cowed,
I will shout my faults out loud,
For I am me, I am myself,
Uncompromising, without stealth.
Laugh all you will, for I will try
To write what I am across the sky.

# The Stag Night

## GUY JENKINSON

A popular perception of university students is that of a pack of drunken wasters whose aspiration to the heights of academe is mere camouflage for several years of parasitic debauchery at the taxpayer's expense. True perhaps in some cases, but, in fact, during his time at university, Tucker had only been on the fringes of the "Magnificent Seven" dining club – a lecherous rabble that terrorised a quiet university city for three years.

Having been informed of his impending nuptials, five of Tucker's one-time fellow students decided on a reunion, to celebrate the traditional "stag" night due to any groom on the eve of his awesome descent into the self-inflicted penury of marriage.

The sixth member was unavailable: a penniless Breton, he had since returned to his Gallic homeland to fulfil his ambition of marrying a rich widow.

This was not the actual night before the event – it was more like a week before. Tucker's intended had made it clear that any unwanted side-effects marring the great day would incur severe civil penalties – like castration with a blunt can-opener.

Nevertheless, it was not long before the festivities had commenced with great dedication. That they had attained a satisfactory level of nostalgia for the misdeeds of misspent youth was evidenced when the participants were urged by the landlord to vacate the "Golden Plover" after a particularly chaotic darts match, which left the regulars ducking friendly fire. The final straw had been an errant projectile that impaled the pub's (stuffed) namesake in its case, over the bar.

Mellowing with the atmosphere – and with the numerous shots of vodka added surreptitiously to his beer – Tucker entered warmly into the spirit of things. Indeed, it was he who proved that pouring Newcastle Amber into the table-football machine did not improve its efficiency – although it led to his party's premature ejection from the "Duke's Head".

Other pubs, a few pies and much drinking followed as evening faded into night.

Having grown out of student-level drinking, by ten-thirty Tucker was starting to wilt. His recollection was hazy of the several rousing choruses of "Eskimo Nell" that had seen them dismissed from the Greyhound hotel. Certainly, he was unaware of his part in ripping the hallowed baize of the Liberal Club's snooker table and hence being carried from there as his comrades fled from a lynch mob of regulars.

Eventually, after imbibing sufficient drink to float, if not a battleship, then at least a light cruiser, the party attempted to wend their way home across the sleeping city. Coming across a seedy tattoo parlour as they staggered drunkenly through the shadowed alleyways of the Old Town, they more or less fell through its still-open doors and demanded service.

In a flash of opportunistic zeal, Tucker's comrades had gleefully decided that he should bear some lasting memento of this, his last few days of bachelorhood. A tattoo was deemed more sophisticated than the traditional debagging and abandonment, handcuffed to some immovable item of street furniture.

Through a fog of alcohol, this seemed like a good idea at the time.

The tattooist had long since closed for the night and was merely putting out the garbage for the morning collection. A slightly built man of East Asian origins and middle years, he balanced the possible consequences of refusing these drunken oafs' demands against the pleasure of fleecing them. Self-preservation coincided with avarice and he ushered them into his studio.

Save for himself, none present spoke the tattooist's native tongue (an obscure dialect of the Cambodian mountains), whilst his command of English was – to be kind – pitiful. An illegal but successful immigrant, since his clandestine arrival in the drum of an imported cement-mixer, he had spent far more time dodging the authorities than acquiring perfection in the language of his unwitting hosts: the Brits. Even so, the fluency of his written English, confined normally to works of fiction like Inland Revenue forms and VAT returns, exceeded that of his spoken word by a comfortable margin. Normally, he accepted instructions from his clients by visual references to standard patterns and images: they pointed, he tattooed, then they paid.

Disgracefully inebriated, of those celebrants who could still speak, one lisped (an effect exacerbated by whisky), one had a stutter (agreed, only under the stress of direct eye contact), two were Brummies and one came from Govan... and Tucker was comatose.

It follows that the multi-cultural negotiations specifying the precise design of tattoo to be executed were somewhat fraught. In short there was a failure of communication. What the merrymakers had intended was the depiction of an item emblematic of their friend's nickname: namely, a rooster. Unfortunately, the slang or vulgar euphemism for the male member has a certain core of commonality that transcends language.

Thus it was that when "Cock" Tucker surfaced the next morning, into a shattering hangover, there upon his chest was an exquisitely detailed depiction of his manhood: fully rigged, gloriously coloured, stretching from throat to navel and, across his lower abdomen, scrotal adornment of commensurate splendour!

# *I found this parcel...*

### PETER CORRIN

I found this parcel on the doorstep; did I miss the postman again?
But no, he won't come out today and it's not got an address to send.
So who's left this parcel out for me? And why did they not knock or ring?
I'm not used, on a Christmas morning, to finding this sort of a thing.

I suppose that I ought to open it; maybe there's a card taped inside,
But I really can't see how it's fastened, not glued, Sellotaped or string-tied.
There's just this smooth golden ribbon tied in an extravagant bow
But look as I might, it seems endless, so if I'm to untie it – just how?

But hang on, I'm making assumptions; maybe this is not meant for me,
It's been left by someone in error for someone other to see.
Hmmm, now that I look a bit closer my name's here all spelt out in gold,
So it appears this mystery parcel is for me from someone untold.

I wish I still believed in Santa; at least I could explain away
This mystery parcel's arrival on *my* doorstep on Christmas Day.
But very few know that I live here in this cottage right out in the sticks
And few people try to come out here when the weather is up to its tricks.

OK, I'll admit it; I'm baffled as to what this parcel might be,
Where it came from and why it is here, how it got here, and why it's for me.
It's heavy but it doesn't rattle, or jingle or make any sound
It doesn't feel threat'ning, or cosy; it's like nothing that I've ever found.

There's no sign of wear on the paper, no single clue where it's from,
No signs of malice aforethought, so I'm sure that it isn't a bomb.
I need to give this a bit more thought; I'll just put it down for a mo'
And make me a cuppa to calm me, before I give it one more go.

Ah, now that I wasn't expecting: the parcel's unwrapping itself!
Very slowly with finite precision, as though being unwrapped by an elf.
I think that I ought to be frightened by this wonderous thing sitting here
But oddly it's really quite calming, and the last thing I'm feeling is fear.

The ribbon has slowly unravelled its beautiful bow on the top
And the ribbon's cascading on all sides; I do hope it's not going to stop.
Now the paper's unfolding, quite slowly, revealing the shape of a box
Made of cedar, if I'm not mistaken, and fitted with two robust locks.

On top of the box, enveloped, is a card with an int'resting shape.
It seems that I have some instructions, and a key for the contents' escape.
The key to the box is quite simple and is beautifully crafted in gold
The card just says 'For Safe Keeping' in letters both striking and bold.

It goes on: ' 'cause I know you won't break it, unlike almost ev'ryone else,
And it needs quite a lot of maintenance; don't just put it up on a shelf.'
Quite awestruck and filled full of wonder I carefully open the box
Prepared to be shocked by the contents and probably blown out my socks
To find what I've wanted for Christmas for too many years since my birth,
A shimmering ingot of crystal with the words etched inside 'Peace on Earth'.

# *Fifty Shades of Marriage*

### BRIAN HUMPHREYS

As he approached the bed, she had no choice but to let him continue. Showered, shaved and smelling of Old Spice, he was the alpha-male, demonstrating his dominance over her. She watched his graceful movements, back and forth, back and forth, his strong hands wrapped firmly around the shaft. Sweat covered his brow. As she watched, he quickened his tempo. He was strong, yet controlled; sweat dripped off the end of his nose; his muscles rippled as he moved. He was panting now; the end was near.

'Lift your legs,' he ordered, his deep rich voice sending shivers down her spine.

She obeyed, contracting her abdominals, finely honed by Zumba and Edam cheese. Her feet lifted from the bedroom carpet, and she held the position in complete submission, her muscles burning, her spine tingling. He quickened his movements even more. She could feel the vibrations from the machine as he moved it back and forth, back and forth until he had finished.

He lifted her bra with his left hand and slipped his right hand inside her knickers. 'I've finished the vacuuming. I'll just put these in the wash, and then I'll make us a drink. How long did the doctor say, before your broken leg's healed?'

*Shortlisted in the 2013
Somerset Short Story Competition*

# The Quicksands of Complacency

## FAITH MOULIN

"What do you mean, you've lost it?" Mr Hathaway was shouting.

Jim had never progressed to first-name terms with his boss. Mr Hathaway kept himself at arm's length, and right at that moment Jim was glad of it.

"I'm afraid it wasn't logged, Mr Hathaway. I don't know why. It should have been logged. It should have been traceable. I mean, it's always traceable, but on this occasion something went wrong."

Mr Hathaway was not about to shrug and say, "Never mind." He did mind. He could feel his neck prickling with anticipation of the block it was going to be on.

"Find out what, man," he yelled, "and come and see me tomorrow!"

Jim slunk out of the office like a dog that's just bitten his master. It wasn't the system that had broken down; it was him. If only he hadn't been worrying about his bloody ex-wife's demands for more maintenance money. If only he hadn't sunk into the quicksands of complacency. He had been sucked under, feet first, standing still for too long.

There were very tight procedures at Sellafield. Especially since Windscale. Especially since Chernobyl. Especially since Fukushima. No one wanted any more scandals in the nuclear industry. As it was, there was a small-scale undercurrent of unease in the community. He couldn't hold on to any girlfriend once he told them where he worked. They were scared of getting contaminated, catching cancer or having babies with two heads.

He went through the scanners every night, just to confirm he hadn't been subject to irradiation. "Clean!" he wanted to shout to the town as he walked home. "Clean as a whistle." He would have liked to blow a whistle and proclaim his cleanness to everyone. The trouble was no one had really trusted the government and now no one trusted the corporation. All they knew were the statistics about cancers in Japan after Nagasaki and Hiroshima – and the quieter statistics about cancers in Cumbria.

Some of the locals didn't help either. Last year the bird-watching fraternity had found out that thirty swallows nesting in the power station were radioactive. It was assumed that they had fed their chicks on mosquitoes from the storage ponds, where radioactive water had bathed and nourished the mosquito larvae. Their metamorphosis didn't change anything. The swallows swallowed them and flew off back to Africa, where no one would turn a Geiger counter on them. The bird-watchers whipped up a frenzy and it was all in the papers, but Jim didn't agree with the fuss. "Where's the harm?" he asked the girl in the supermarket. "It's only birds. It's not people."

Sellafield had said they would fill in the ponds and make the swallows work harder for their supper. "There was no breach," the PR department's soft voice had soothed, smooth and smug. "No one is to blame."

Jim was to blame this time, though. He couldn't deny it. It was his job to sort the waste – not the spent fuel, of course; that was dealt with by scientists with white coats and nice cars. He had a brown coat and a clapped-out old banger. He had the job of sorting and disposing of less hazardous waste: the discarded gloves, masks, overalls and other protective gear worn by the better-paid people who were working closer to danger. That was what he had tried to tell the women he met for dates. He wasn't any risk. But they never believed it. To them the forbidding fortress was every bit as scary as Count Dracula's dark castle – sinister, sepulchral, looming over the landscape, excluding light, exuding evil.

He might not work there much longer, he thought. This was surely a sackable offence. It wouldn't matter so much if there were other jobs to go to, but there really wasn't much around Sellafield and his bloody ex-wife would still be after her pound of flesh. If he moved away he would lose contact with his kids.

He applied his mind to the problem. What had happened? How had tons of radioactive material turned up at the landfill site? More to the point, how had it ended up crossing the North Sea? He couldn't explain to Mr Hathaway how a whole container-load of low-grade waste, his own personal responsibility, had ended up being burnt in Norway as environmentally friendly fuel.

Next day he reported to Mr Hathaway's office and was glad to see a calmer man sitting benignly behind his desk, sipping coffee out of a paper cup. That cup could end up in Norway, but that would be all right. It was OK to burn the paper waste from an English nuclear power station in a Norwegian incinerator to fuel a more sustainable power station over there. It squared the circle. Neat. Sweet. Hygienic. The cup shouldn't be contaminated with any trace of radioactivity, so that was fine. It was quite environmentally friendly really and only slightly ironic.

"Have you brought me an answer, Jim?" asked Mr Hathaway.

"I think I have an explanation," Jim began. He would have liked to say 'sir' to show his respect, but it wasn't in the Sellafield work culture so he just went on as deferentially as he could. "I always log the consignments of waste on a spreadsheet."

Mr Hathaway nodded. So far, so good.

"I think one day there was a power failure. We do get them sometimes. Something to do with the switching, isn't it, Mr Hathaway?"

Mr Hathaway frowned slightly but nodded him on.

"I was working on the spreadsheet and the power cut just turned the computer off momentarily. I think the information I had just entered must have got lost."

Mr Hathaway looked slightly less benign now. Jim went on:

"It's assumed that where no code is entered the waste is OK for recycling or landfill. I think I might have failed to check it. I probably should have checked the spreadsheet, but I think that load just went off with the ordinary waste." Jim looked up from his feet to Mr Hathaway's face. It was thoughtful but inscrutable. He started up again nervously: "It didn't have a code by it, that consignment. It should have had the fan blades radiation warning symbol, but it had nothing by it. That's why it went to the tip. It should have gone to the Hazardous Waste area instead. The code just got lost somehow."

"Lost?" Mr Hathaway asked. "How are we going to present this 'loss' to the wider world, Jim?"

Jim didn't know. Jim thought he wasn't really paid to answer that question. It was the boss's call, that one. Mr Hathaway, on the other hand, was inclined towards the thought that Jim had got him into this mess and Jim should get him out.

"I'm sorry, Mr Hathaway. I don't know," said Jim. "I suppose the public has to accept that we're only human. The waste on this occasion just got lost."

Jim met his ex-wife in the supermarket a month later. She looked well and was in some very smart new clothes. He noticed the new leather bag and the dangly earrings.

"I'm glad I bumped into you," she said, smoothing her hair with a hand that was armed with gold rings.

*That's uncharacteristic of you,* thought Jim, but he just smiled.

"I'm going to have to have a bit more money, Jim. You haven't answered the solicitor's letter, have you?"

Jim shook his head. "It's difficult," he said, but he felt at peace. She couldn't get at him now. She would have to earn her own money. He was living in a dark, damp basement flat in a cold, shady street which faced into the bitter north winds. She had cleaned him out. He had no car, no bike, no television, no telephone, no comfortable chair, no comfortable anything, but here was his comfort. Cold comfort, but some comfort. The stick of truth was a good thing to beat her with.

*You can whistle for more money,* he thought, and the thought consoled him like a mother's cuddle, like a lover's embrace, like his children's bedtime hugs and wet kisses.

"I've lost my job," he said.

# *Howzat?*

## SALLY ANN NIXON

"Hi, ho, and away we go!"

George sang blearily down the village street, stumbling to inspect the green before the morning. A cricketing BIG NAME was coming to the Magna Fete and it fell to George to make the last checks.

It was a cool, clear night but George sweated and struggled, avoiding Somerset Council's pothole preservation scheme which took up most of the road.

"Hi, ho, and down we go!"

George swore, tripped, righted himself and came up hard against the churchyard lychgate. He clung to the fretwork, testing his ricked ankle and his banged knee, for a sick moment fearing that his captaincy of the Magna cricket team was jeopardised – something even Margaret had not been able to accomplish. George squinted at the trees on the far side of the pitch.

"Bloody potholes. Bloody council tax..."

George muttered a tirade against the old, the young, the feckless and the foreign, as he limped towards the pavilion. He slumped on the steps, scrabbled for his torch, eventually weaving a thin beam across the immaculate pitch. All was well. The beam wavered from side to side and nothing showed to disquiet George's fuddled mind. Absentmindedly, he scratched at his upper lip where Margaret had made him shave off his moustache.

"Makes you look old, George. Dated. No one has them. Only tramps and that sort. Smarten up."

Margaret had changed. She'd gone to Slimmer's World, then had her mousey bob styled and streaked. Her new wardrobe had cost a pretty penny. Money that George had earmarked for the 'George

Wandlesworth Cup', for the cricket club. George didn't like the changes at all.

Margaret had started going out, too. Without him. The book circle, the writers' group, even the sisterhood club, for God's sake. Not content with a G&T at the Bull, like a decent Englishwoman, Margaret now demanded Prosecco at the Bistro. Never at home. No meals cooked. George felt sidelined. He wished he had his pipe, but Margaret had stopped that. All his harmless little pleasures – gone. What little food Margaret cooked was all nouveau this and Jamie's that. God, what he'd give for a steaming slice of steak and kidney pud. Or roast pork, crackling and apple sauce.

George shed a dribbly tear of self-pity. When had his compliant little Margaret, always so sure that he knew best, become this assertive, undutiful dragon of a woman? Enough! Last night George had decided to reclaim his manhood. Flushed with the recollection, George staggered up, clung to a fence post and thrust an imaginary sword starwards.

"For God, for Magna, cricket and for George!" he cried.

"For me," he whispered, lowering his sword to the ground.


Again the torch swept over the pitch where he had laboured early that morning. No one remarked old George with his wheelbarrow full of tools and sacking, solemnly levelling and rolling the pitch boundary by the trees, where the smooth grass met the rough ground. A dim and shady spot. No one walked there. Out of the way. There, some feet down, George's dragon could rest in peace.

# *You Can Try Too Hard*

## JENNY MURPHY

For some inexplicable reason, care workers like myself overcompensate for people's disabilities. Is it the guilt of having so much more choice, aspiration and material wealth that does it? Does an endless round of jolliness up to the actual day replace the one thing that most of my people want: to be included in a family? I think not, but we still do it, year-on-year.

The Christmas party is intended to be the pinnacle of our efforts, including a visit from Santa when everyone receives a gift. This may seem a little childish, but a large number of the group still believe, despite their advancing years.

Brenda is not a believer but she is determined not to lose out. Five foot nine in all directions, she enters the room clutching Eddie, her chosen companion, in a vice-like grip. He isn't arguing but, there again, he is no fool.

The first part of the evening is completed in time for the buffet supper, laid optimistically on the covered pool table. It only takes a moment for Brenda to circumnavigate the spread, collecting generous portions of chocolate cake, sausage rolls and sandwiches. Eddie is slightly less fortunate in his attempt to hoover up food, having temporarily misplaced his false teeth.

The food soon disappears leaving no evidence that it actually existed, and now comes the moment we have all been waiting for, the less-than-spectacular entrance of Santa, to the tuneless rendition of *Rudolph, the Red-Nosed Reindeer*.

This year's choice of Santa is particularly poor. He is nervous, flabby, and sweating profusely under his cheap costume, and he does not seem very keen on being enthusiastically sat upon. Slowly the gifts are distributed and the exercise appears to have come to an end when out of the shadows steps Brenda. 'Where's my gift?' she asks while slightly invading the personal space of our shrinking Santa.

Feeling brave, I step forward. 'Santa's little helpers have made a mistake. Let's all have another chorus of *Rudolph* while I check what they are doing.'

Having finished the washing-up, they are having a much-needed mulled wine break and are no use at all. I search the back room for a suitable gift and can only find a spare chocolate orange. Hastily, I pop this into a bag and slide back into the room.

Brenda steps forward menacingly, and Santa anxiously hands over the bag. She looks inside, sees the chocolate and grabs Santa by the throat. 'Don't you know I'm a bloody diabetic?' With this, she plants a punch firmly on his nose. Santa staggers back and falls into the lopsided Christmas tree as he tries to avoid further blows.

Anger dissipated, Brenda polishes off the chocolate orange and drags Eddie onto the dance floor. The music is back on, and as dancing resumes, my thoughts are with the injured Santa who has disappeared, costume and all.

It looks like I will need a replacement Santa for next year; preferably an ex-boxer with his own costume and a little more courage!

# The Blue of the Kingfisher

### VICTORIA HELEN TURNER

On a still summer morning towards the end of the last century, on a river where trees overhung the water's edge, gazing shyly yet vainly at the reflection of their leafy-green dresses in the shimmering blueness, a young woman lay sleepily where the close-growing peppermint was thick to the ground, making a pillow for the beautiful young head, thick, dark curly hair, bound in an orange ribbon, intermingling with the pungent peppermint. The face delicate, red-lipped, thick black lashes concealed eyes which a moment before had been heavy, lulled to sleep by the lullaby of humming bees and the hot stillness and the occasional splash of a moorhen.

The girl's eyes, a clear grey, suddenly flicked open. A gleam of brilliant blue flashed across her sight; it was a kingfisher and she knew she must follow it. She rose dreamlike from her peppermint bank and followed the gleam of blue along the river. It seemed at times to wait for her as if it wanted her to catch up with it. The humming of the bees grew louder and the song of the birds was the most beautiful the girl had ever heard. As she came nearer to the kingfisher, a strange sweet tune, as if played on pipes, grew louder. The melody seemed familiar, yet she knew she'd never heard it before; the tune called to her to follow. The colour of the flowers grew more brilliant as she passed by, bluebells almost caressing her flowing orange skirts, which belled out with the gentle breeze from the river, and the fragrance of the flowers and plants became overpowering with their sweetness, and as the growing things smelled sweeter, so the strange pipe melody grew sweeter, louder, and more wild, and the blue of the kingfisher grew more and more brilliant.

The small wild creatures, usually so shy, peeped from the undergrowth, and hopped and skipped around her feet, completely unafraid, dancing as she now did to the strange music of the pipes. On the river's edge, she saw the player of the pipes, the panpipes; he swished his hairy goat legs in the water, in time with his music. The kingfisher was perched on his shoulder, and the bird's blueness grew brighter and brighter until it was almost blinding.

The player of the pipes turned his head towards the girl; he continued playing, but his green eyes, the eyes of eternal spring, a green so perfect it dimmed the green perfection of the earth around him, seemed to beckon her, as did his melody, whispering in a voice older than time – "come, follow me, you are one of those rare ones who See, come with me and see the Truth."

He rose from the riverbank, still playing, and all the small creatures followed him, the kingfisher still perched on his shoulder. He walked beneath the trees, but turned again to look at the girl, his handsome ugly face with its goat's horns and the message "come" in his beautiful green eyes. The girl picked up her orange skirts and ran after the player of the pipes and the blue of the kingfisher. She knew she must follow his call. She at last caught up with him, breathless, and clutched the hairy arm of the player of the pipes and cried desperately, "I'm coming too!"

"Where are you going, Ann?" said a voice quietly.

The hairy arm Ann was clutching turned into a sleeve of Harris Tweed, and she looked up into the beautiful eyes of her lover, the green of eternal spring.

"I'm going with you," she whispered.

The young man put his arms around her, and then cupped her lovely face in his hands. "But *where* are you going with me, Ann?" he asked.

Ann stared at him steadily, seeming to hear again that strange melody of the panpipes, and to smell with ecstasy the overpowering fragrance of the flowers around them, as she heard the humming of the bees, the glorious birdsong. Then quietly, gently, like the sigh of the breeze along the river, the secret of the player of the pipes, the secret of the kingfisher and the brilliance and beauty around her – the truth of what she had been seeking stole into her dreamer's mind and her heart was at last at peace. The truth was love, and love was the only Truth. When her dream, if dream it was, had changed from a god to a man, she had thought of him as her lover, and he was – she loved him, and had always loved him. Patient Charles, the dream she sought had been beside her all the time.

"I'm going with you through life, Charles, that's *where* I'm going, because I love you, I've always loved you."

Charles smiled, and the sun shot golden streamers through the trees, like yellow ribbons on their leafy green dresses. He bent his head and kissed her gently, as gently as the melody of the pipes.

"I've waited a long time to hear you say that – dearest Ann," he whispered against her hair. "I know you saw something... you've no need to tell me what it was. Mother always said you had the Second Sight, but whatever or whoever it was you saw, I'm grateful too, because it's given me your love."

"You've always had my love, Charles. This... dream... only showed me what I should have realised long ago, that what I longed to find was already mine."

"I know you're a dreamer, Ann, and though my fancies can never be as fantastic as your own, I'll always understand them, even if I can't share them."

Ann smiled up at the man who had waited patiently for more than three years, down-to-earth Charles, yet with enough imagination to see that it was he she had always loved. Had she really seen the player of the pipes or heard his melody? Charles was her dream and he was real enough, but maybe the dream was real too, because in the distance she could still see the brilliant blue of the kingfisher!

# FIFTY-WORD STORIES

## *Doing One's Duty*

### LYNDA HOTCHKISS

"Keep your head down."

Jim did not move. He'd said he would come home after this madness ended.

"Over the top."

Jim could not move. Rooted to the spot, he'd watched his comrades follow orders, remains of some of them at his feet.

"Aim. Fire."

Jim's not going home.

## *How History Could Have Changed*

### LYNDA HOTCHKISS

The drum roll stopped and the man in a black hood stepped forward, hand extended for payment. The girl placed a silver coin into his palm, then rested her slender neck on the block. The axe flashed.

"Stop!" came a voice from behind. "Anne Boleyn has been spared. Oops!"

## *Creation – Yorkshire Style*

### GUY JENKINSON

In t'beginning there were nowt, then t'Lord said, "Leet oop!" an' tha' could see for miles.

During t'following week 'Ee made night, day, 'eaven, earth, watter an' t'rest – including all t'fish, birds, insects, animals an' owt else needed.

'Ee finished t'job wi' Adam an' 'is missis.

T'rest were 'istory, sithee.

*Placed SECOND in the 2013*
*Somerset Short Story Competition*

# Press Any Key

### BRIAN HUMPHREYS

Angus flared his nostrils before the bathroom mirror, studying the undergrowth like a young David Attenborough. His wife's voice boomed up the stairs. 'Do you have any plans today?'

Angus wandered downstairs. 'I was thinking of defoliating.'

'There's a sale on at Dixons.'

'They've always got a sale on. You've a toaster and microwave; what more do you want?'

'A computer.'

'A computer?' The word stuck in his throat like a fishbone. 'Why in God's name...'

'Don't bring God into this, and while we're on the subject, don't think I haven't noticed the Bible on your bedside cabinet. Why are you reading *that*?'

'I'm cramming for my finals, if you must know. I'd rather go non-smoking than smoking.'

Rose shook her head. 'Stop worrying about the afterlife, you're only sixty. Life's for living.'

'Anyway, *you* can talk.'

'Yes dear, but only because God gave me vocal cords.' Rose regarded religion with the same disgust as something you might find growing at the back of a fridge.

'Don't think I haven't noticed the book on *your* bedside cabinet, Rose. Since when have you been interested in decorating? There's only one shade of grey, certainly not fifty.'

Rose decided that ignorance was bliss. Old age had wrapped around Angus like an old cardigan. When they had married, the ten-year age gap had meant nothing, but now, it was wider than the Grand Canyon.

In the car, Rose passed Angus a tissue. 'Half your brain's hanging out of your left nostril. At least push it back in; it might come in handy, one day.'

Using his index finger, Angus completed brain surgery and started the car. 'Where to?'

'You know where, Dixons. Betty's bought a computer, and I want one.'

'Betty's got piles; do you want some of those?'

'And how do you know she's got piles?'

'My memory might be failing, and my brain might be falling out of my nose, but there's nothing wrong with my ears. You and Betty talk about her piles so often, I'm surprised they don't have Christian names.'

Rose scowled. 'Could you try harder to find a gear? Otherwise, by the time *we* arrive, they'll be sold out.'

'Wouldn't that be a shame?'

Half way to Dixons, Rose broke the silence. 'Many people enjoy computers, and Betty said there's plenty of free advice on the internet.'

'So, let me get this straight. If we spend hundreds of pounds on a computer, printer, ink and paper, we'll get *free* advice?'

Inside Dixons, Rose made straight for Jason, the young assistant. 'Can you show me some computers?'

'Certainly; is it an upgrade you want?'

Rose looked at Angus. 'Yes please, something with more memory.'

'How much more?'

'Remembering yesterday would be good,' said Angus. 'Anything else, I'll consider a bonus.'

'Do you want two gigs of memory, or three?'

'Just two,' said Angus, 'we've only got a small bungalow.'

Rose received a text, and read the message. Jason sensed another sales opportunity.

'Madam...'

'Please, call me Rose.'

'Rose, your phone is a little old-fashioned; could I interest you in our latest BlackBerry? It's only £30 a month *and* you get free texts.'

'Hear that, Rose? If we pay £30 a month for a phone we don't need, we'll get free texts! Isn't technology wonderful?'

Jason persevered. 'Rose, do you tweet?'

'No, but she farts a lot,' said Angus, receiving an elbow in his ribs.

'Shut up, you're embarrassing me.'

'Rose, do you know which computer you want?'

'Yes. Last weekend, you sold my friend Betty a computer. I'd like one the same, but slightly better.'

Jason tried to remember Betty. 'Can you describe her?'

'She looks like Gollum from *Lord of the Rings*,' said Angus, dodging another elbow, 'and she walks like him too, on account of her piles.'

After checking last week's sales, Jason found a slightly more advanced model for Rose. 'Would you like personal surfing lessons?'

Rose imagined Jason in a wetsuit, her cheeks turning a dusky red.

Angus gave Jason his new and improved death-stare, level six. 'Personal lessons won't be necessary, but we'll need this... *thing* put in our car.'

Reaching the age of sixty without ever having touched a computer or a mobile phone, let alone actually using one, was a badge that Angus wore with pride: a Victoria Cross in the face of his enemy, the silicon chip.

While Rose paid the bill, Angus memorised the display computer connections: green to green, purple to purple, black to black.

With the computer in the boot, Angus searched for a gear. 'Well, that's two hours of my life I won't get back. I've not had that much fun since... since...'

Rose smirked. 'I told you we should have gone for more memory.'

With gritted teeth, Angus set up the computer and turned it on. Rose had a glint in her eye. Even if Jason's flirting was the cause, Angus sensed an opportunity for... well, he was never one to initiate... matters, but he wanted to let Rose know how he was feeling. The computer instructed: *enter password*. Under Rose's scrutiny, Angus typed in capital letters: *MY PENIS*. The computer screen changed: *password not long enough*. Rose burst out laughing.

Angus cursed. 'Just give me an hour, and I'll have this... thing... ready for use.' Neither of them believed that for a second.

'I'm going surfing with Betty. I'll see you later.'

With Rose out of the house, Angus phoned Dixons. 'Jason? It's Angus. You sold a computer to my wife Rose this morning, and offered personal lessons. We need your help *now*, because *MY PENIS* isn't long enough.'

Jason fainted.

When it came to technology, Angus was lost. His eyes flicked from the computer screen to the keyboard, again and again. In desperation, he phoned an IT helpline. 'I need help, *MY PENIS* isn't long enough.'

'I'm sorry, sir, you've dialled a wrong number. This is an IT helpline, not a medical helpline.'

'Let me explain. I tried to set up my computer using *MY PENIS...*'

'It's much easier if you use your fingers and thumbs.'

Angus explained about the password.

'I see,' laughed the IT man. 'You had me worried for a moment. My name's Marty, what's yours?'

'Angus.'

'Right, let's start at the beginning. Who's your service provider?'

'British Gas.'

Working the IT helpline bored Marty, but every now and then, along came a silver surfer to brighten his day. 'Angus, what message is displayed onscreen?'

'*Press any key to continue.* I can see lots of keys: *sleep, power, delete, shift, backspace,* but I can't find the *any* key.'

'Press the large *enter* key. It's on the right-hand side. What's the message now?'

'*Reset password.*'

'Angus, I want you to type in the box: *incorrect.*'

'Why?'

'So that in future, when you forget your password, the computer screen will display: *your password is incorrect.*'

'Brilliant, I like your thinking, Marty.'

'Now, can you see the internet icon? It's a large blue "e". Double-click it, and we'll do some surfing.'

Angus shuddered at the thought. 'No thanks, I've got some defoliating to do.'

'How old are you, Angus?'

'Just turned sixty.'

'Born in the 1950s? That must have been a tough time.'

Angus warmed to Marty. 'It was tough. If it wasn't for my best friend, Danny Zebrasky, I don't think I'd have survived.'

'What's he doing now?'

'Don't know, we lost touch years ago.'

'That's a shame. Tell me, Angus, what was the first record you ever bought?'

'*Tell Laura I Love Her.*' Angus recalled the thrill of buying his first single. 'It was a ballad about two lovers.'

'Yes, Laura and Tommy.'

'You know it?'

'I'm listening to it right now. All the songs ever recorded, and videos of the artists, are on the internet, you can watch them for free; and while we've been chatting, I've found 760 Danny Zebraskys, and some are pictured. But be careful when searching for friends on-line; don't open any flashing adverts.'

'I won't be watching flashing adverts, or any pornography.'

'Angus, sometimes things just pop up, unexpectedly.'

'Not in our house they don't.'

'Do you have perhaps one last question?'

'Yes; do e-mails get delivered on Sundays?'

Rose slammed the front door and shouted upstairs, 'Is it working?'

Angus wandered downstairs. 'Almost.'

'Well, don't bother. Betty and me sat surfing for ages and I've never been so bored.'

'Never mind. Perhaps you'll develop piles? Then you'll have something else in common.'

'You'd like that, wouldn't you?'

Angus imagined Rose walking like Gollum. 'Shall I put the computer in the spare bedroom, alongside your unused rowing machine and cross trainer?'

Angus hummed *Three Steps to Heaven* as he climbed the stairs, whistled *Tell Laura I Love Her* as he positioned the computer near a socket, and sang *Do You Want to Know a Secret* as he wandered downstairs.

He kept from Rose his new-found joy of surfing, and also forgot to mention that he'd traced his childhood sweetheart. Ignorance was bliss, he decided.

# Compton Bishop Churchyard

PETER CORRIN

Just for one extended moment
No voice could be heard
No dog barked
No cow lowed
No lamb bleated
No pigeon cooed
No wind blew
No tree rustled
No bird sang
No branch creaked
No thing disturbed the settled silence
And as everything held its breath

I could hear the clouds float by

# Wait

## BARBARA EVANS

I wait and wait, he won't be long... I hope he won't be long....

There are lovely leaves lying in corners, crushed and whole. They lie piled and layered, crisping golden and brown with lime fringes. They flap away from fast feet. They are tucked into corners and blown along edges. They lodge in nooks and crannies where the wind has stuffed them. Vellum-shaded, they wait there like untidy piles of aged yellowing paper.

I sip my tea; it is weak. The teabag will not let out the taste. I stir and beat it round the pot, but the searing water cannot release the full flavour, the green-tea taste. Its little leafy core is still un-brewed as I wait and wait. I stir again. The teabag bursts and clouds of small specks swirl around the pot.

The window reaches to the floor; I can be seen from top to toe. I am inside, I am outside. He will see me here. My blue bag and my handbag are visible to all, but the glass is a magic screen. The passing multitude are oblivious. I am like a fish half-hidden beneath the glittering reflection of a stream's surface.

A man presses his face to the glass not three feet from me, but he looks right past me. I am invisible and ignorable like goods in a shop window, seen and forgotten. I am on show, but the man looks only into the room beyond my table. The people inside are drinking coffee, drinking tea, eating toast. Many, many people come and go. They stop for a break, or go to their meetings. I stay where I am. I wait and wait but he doesn't come.

I can see the bus-station doors, they open, they close; they open, they close. Passengers pass through. The stream doesn't stop. Tall people, thin people, lovely ladies, large ladies and big and little men. They come and they go. The café is the first thing they see. He will see me here.

I have come into town especially to see him. I sent him a text. I told him I would be here and I expect he will come as soon as he is free. This is a special place for us. This is where we first met. This is where we shared a table when all the others were full.

"May I join you?" he said. He had the lasagne like me. I had nearly finished mine; it was delicious. After that I don't think I tasted it any more. My senses became dulled as love blossomed. It was pretty much love at first sight. Now we meet and love, our passion is overflowing. It washes over us and it flows into every part of our lives. It is as natural as nature. It is fundamental and fulfilling. No one else exists. The world is one with us and empty of all but us. Oh, how I love him!

I am pregnant. I think he knows, I think he has guessed that our love has borne fruit. It could spoil everything. I don't think he will be able to live with that. He will not be able to share his life with another child in another relationship. It could be a disaster for him. It could be the end. How I wish it was not so!

How I wish I could rewind this story to a place where we went beyond ourselves into another world. When our love transcended time and place, propriety and purpose. Where love was as unconscious as breathing and belonged to our being. Then love was new and easy and consequence did not exist, or else it disappeared into the mist.

My eyes begin to fill and overflow, tears dropping onto the serviette and raising blobs and wrinkles to pucker it out of shape. I don't want to be seen. I don't want these tears to flow down my face. They will paint me with a shiny gloss, showing me up, exposing my hidden unhappiness.

People are beginning to turn to look at me. I feel conspicuous. I keep my head down, gazing at every little smear on the table, every little scrape in the wood, glass and metal in my view. I see every little bit of gathering grime, damage and decay.

I rise to my feet and I scrape the chair back. It is loud and echoing. I tumble the knife to the floor, and reach for my bags as my tears rain down on them. People start towards me, concerned, but I don't want their help, I don't want their intervention, I don't want anyone at all. I want to go home.

Home is something I can be certain of, home is security. I stumble, I stagger. I blunder towards the door. I push instead of pulling and my hands feel the impact. I wrench it open and tumble over the threshold and start off towards the beckoning bus station doors.

The bus starts off. It wobbles, jolts, hisses and bangs and suddenly brakes. I am tossed about and thrown this way and that. It is a cruel addition to my pain. I sit on the high seats at the back, because no one will turn around to look at me up here. Soon I am home.

I turn the key in the front door and I feel as if life is over. It has ended. I don't want to continue. I don't want to live without you. I stand in the porch and loud sobs start from my mouth and my tears flow freely once more. I stand stuck, unmoving in the middle of my misery. I don't know how to put my bags down, or how to kick off my shoes. I feel my legs weaken and my unhappiness unfolds and spreads as I sink onto the little chair. The inner door opens. He is here!

He has been waiting for me, here at home! He raises me to my feet and enfolds me, kissing my hair, my head, my face. Kissing my tears away. He murmurs reassurance. "It will be all right," he says. "Don't worry any more, it will all be OK."

I don't know yet what he means but I lean on those words. I lean heavily on the idea of hope that he has now instilled in me. His love erases all, and peace comes over me. I am back home where I belong, where we belong. Where home is held wholly in his arms. Where forever fits inside a kiss.

# *Storytelling*

## SALLY ANN NIXON

It is storytime at the library.
I first did this so long ago.
It has changed so much over the years,
From listen with Mother to listen with Gran.

Then they sat in a neat circle,
Angel faces, hands folded in laps.
Intent on what you said, or read or whispered,
Watching your face, watching the picture book.

Times do change. They wander now.
"It's television's done it," we complain.
"No listening skills and poor attention span."
Each session made of quick, short tales and song.

There was a time when we had weekly stories.
The children came each time and tales went on
From week to week. It made it so much easier.
A long tale interspersed with rhyme and song

And yet, and yet. The triumph when they pay attention.
A breakthrough with a poem, joke or rhyme.
Suddenly something grabs them and they listen,
Moving with you, not against you.

This is proper story time.

# A Fisherman's Tale

### LYNDA HOTCHKISS

Rose Enderby patted her hair into place as she looked into a small scrap of mirror that was propped up on the spotless mantelpiece of her humble home. To the left was a glass jar containing a few coins, and on the right two similar jars, one with lots of pebbles in and the other containing one solitary stone. She felt a tug at her skirts and looked down to see her little boy, George, smiling up at her. He was nearly five years old and the only child that had survived. He was the reason Ralph had gone to sea.

"Look, Georgie," said Rose, lifting him up in her arms. "The last pebble."

She put her hand into the jar and grasped the stone. She held it out to her son, who reached out for it. He dropped it into the full jar, and flung his arms round her neck.

Ralph had left a jar of money for her and the boy while he was away, and the other two jars for her to keep track of time, one pebble out of one jar and into the other every day. Now the last pebble had been removed and Ralph was due home.

With George's hand in hers, Rose strode confidently down the cobbled streets towards the dock, holding tightly under her chin the black shawl that covered her head. Other women were stepping out of their homes and taking the same walk to wait for their menfolk to return. They didn't speak to each other, just a nod of acknowledgement as they fell into step. Soon the town rang to the sound of clogs on cobbles as this indomitable army of women made their way to the quayside.

They gathered along the water's edge in small groups, their children standing silently by their sides. Everyone stared out towards the horizon waiting to see the first boat home.

The boats started to straggle back in twos and threes. As each crew discharged their cargo of fresh fish, and their pay was doled into their hands, their families would run down to meet them, hugging and crying with relief that their men were home again.

The crowds that had gathered so quietly left for their meagre homes in great spirits, leaving just a handful waiting and straining to see a mast on the horizon, hoping that the next boat that docked was the one their men were on.

By teatime, only seven women stood on the dockside. They walked towards each other, and held hands. Tears were running down one or two cheeks, and some were wringing their hands or biting their lips with worry. A middle-aged lady fell to her knees and started to pray.

Rose was worrying about Ralph but she stood ramrod-straight, choking back the tears. Her son shifted from one foot to the other, but he too waited patiently, following his mother's example.

With the light fading, someone tapped Rose's shoulder. "C'mon, love."

Rose turned and looked into the kind face of the skipper's wife.

"No point waiting any longer. They won't come in tonight. They have to wait for the morning tide. Take yersel' off home and tuck that wee laddie up warm."

Rose took one last look into the dark, willing herself to see a small light that indicated a boat was heading home, and then nodded. She scooped up George, who put his head on her shoulder and closed his eyes. Slowly she made her way home.

The storm had sent them off course, and now the skipper had locked himself in the bridge room, along with three bottles of aniseed brandy. Ralph regretted signing on for this trip as he had expected to go fishing and then come back home. Instead, the skipper had pulled up the nets after two or three days, saying he had been told of somewhere that teemed with fish. They sailed for a day or so, the skipper imbibing more of the brandy than was good for him, but they met with a similar-sized boat, and the crew were sent down below. Only the skipper and the apprentice stayed aloft, and about thirty minutes later, Ralph and his two colleagues were back at their stations.

"Time to head home, lads," the skipper shouted through the small window, and the boat turned about.

The wind picked up again, and the boat started to pitch and roll. Suddenly there was a crashing sound, and the boat started to list.

"Shall I check the cargo?" Ralph shouted, his hands already releasing the locks on the hatches. "I think it's shifted."

The skipper shouted, "No! Leave it be!"

Pointing at the loosened hatch cover, Ralph hollered, "It won't take a minute. It's causing us to take on water on the starboard side."

He lifted the hatch cover and started to go down to where they stacked the fish in special holds, packed with ice and held in place with wooden slats. Then there was a scream, a bang and everything went black.

When he awoke, it was calm, and the sun was trying to poke through. His head ached. He sat up and squinted around but no one was on deck. He waved at the bridge, but that too appeared deserted. He made his way below deck but the bunks were empty. The mess was empty – except for Shorty.

Shorty was acting mate on the *Noah*, and had been for the last four years. He was a quiet man until the drink got him. That was when he would spend time in the clink, and would have to wait for the next fishing trip. Now he was very quiet, an ice-pick in his back. Ralph turned and vomited on the floor. He had never seen a dead body like Shorty before, and who had done this?

He moved to the skipper's cabin and knocked respectfully. No one answered.

Cautiously opening the door, he was taken aback at the state of the desk and floor – crumpled navigational maps, ripped-up charts and empty brandy bottles. The small cash box that the skipper kept in a drawer was open on the bunk – and empty.

The next morning, Rose and George again made the walk to the harbour. They waited with a couple of others but no one spoke. At dusk, only Rose stood watching, little George by her side. It was only when George started to cry that she realised he needed to go home. She took his hand and sadly went back alone.

She repeated her vigil for the next three days, and no one else joined her. As she stared out at the vast expanse of ocean, her thoughts raced as to where her husband might be. She didn't dare think that he would never return. How would she cope without him, and what about little Georgie?

*Of course he'll come home!* she would tell herself sternly. *Ralph would never leave you, and he loves our son so much. He will be here... soon, soon.*

Ralph could hear someone moving about on deck. Swiftly and silently he went up top and waited. A shadow appeared on the planking and Ralph prepared himself to pounce.

"Gotcher!" he called as he leapt on a creeping figure. There was a squeal, followed by sobbing and a plea for mercy. Ralph drew back and realised he had caught hold of Arthur, the boat's apprentice lad.

"Don't 'urt me, mister," said Arthur with a sniff. "It ain't my fault. I ain't done nuffing!"

"What do you mean, lad? I won't hurt you. What happened? Where's the skipper?"

Arthur looked over his shoulder before answering. "Skipper's gone mad! He was fighting with Shorty and I fink 'e killed 'im!"

Ralph nodded, knowing that was indeed true. "Where's the skipper now, Arthur?"

"I don't know!" wailed Arthur. "I just keep walking about 'opin' 'e don't find me. Last I saw of 'im, 'e was going down to the lower decks with an axe."

"And Billy? Where's Billy?" Ralph asked.

Arthur shook his head and pointed over the side.

Ralph took in a deep breath. "Go into the bridge room, lock yourself in and see if you can find a heading. We have to go home. Can you do that?"

Arthur nodded, and he suddenly gave a smile. "You're gonna let me take the wheel?"

"I'm not just letting you take the wheel, Arthur, I need you to. I've got to go and find the skipper."

Ralph had given the boy something to hope for, even though the main mast had been damaged in the recent storm.

At that point there came a crashing sound and a maniacal laugh. More crashing, the sound of metal on wood, and then the boat juddered.

"We're taking on water!" Ralph shouted, reaching for a lifebelt. The clips were empty.

Grabbing Arthur's hand, he ran towards the back of the boat, where a solitary lifebelt was lying forlornly on the deck. He pushed it over Arthur's head and told him to jump. "Better to jump and try swimming than get trapped on this bucket," he said. "God be with you, lad."

He never saw Arthur jump over the side. He went in search of the skipper, and hopefully another lifebelt.

Rose continued to stand on the quayside every day for the next two weeks. George was in school now, so her vigil was a solitary task. Everyone knew why she was there, knew what had happened, but no one made the effort to talk to her, to help her in her pitiful hope that her husband would come home.

She didn't stay as long now, spending the evenings working at the laundry to buy food and pay the rent on their meagre fisherman's cottage, but now the landlord wanted her and the boy out. He had another family who needed the house and they had a skipper to work for.

Rose knew things were stacking up against her. Her family were dead, and his refused to acknowledge her, claiming she was not a suitable wife for their son. Ralph had been cut off by his farming father the day he married Rose, though there had been a letter on George's third birthday, saying that Ralph's family would raise the boy. Ralph had been so angry at the very idea, and that was when they had moved to find work, settling in this little fishing town, where they had been happy for the last year or so.

Ralph clung to the side of the boat and tried to see where he was. All he could see was water and sky – acres of it. His legs were cold now, and his fingers were finding it hard to hold on to this section of hull. His head ached still from the blow he had received when the skipper went on the rampage.

The hold had been full of gin and brandy, tobacco and cigars: illicit cargo that was going to cost every one of them their lives. Shorty was dead, killed by the skipper in a drunken rage. Billy had gone overboard, either by accident or with the skipper's help. Little Arthur – well, he was alive last time Ralph saw him, but that had been two, or was it three, days ago? Just before the boat sank. Luckily for Ralph, the skipper's handy work with an axe had caused it to break up as the waves sucked it down. This small piece of broken planking had bobbed up in front of his face, and he had grabbed it with great hope that he would get back home to his dear sweet Rose, and their darling boy.

He felt dizzy and sick. His lips were dry but he dared not drink the salty water that was all around him. He tried to paddle in what he thought was the direction of home, but then he got too tired, followed by too cold, and now he was too exhausted to think, even to dream. All he could do was imagine Rose standing waiting for him, with little Georgie by her side.

"Tell her I tried to come home," he said to a passing seabird. "Tell her I tried, I really really tried!"

Jack shouted at his crew to heave to. He pointed ahead of their little fishing boat to where a piece of broken hull was floating on the waves. They pulled it aboard, and Jack stared down at the name of the unfortunate vessel – *Noah*.

Rose stood on the top of the hill, looking out across the harbour to where the sea caressed the sky. She held her son's hand tightly, as if he might disappear from her side if she let go.

"Dadda's not coming home, is he, Mammy?" said George.

Rose felt a lump in her throat, and shook her head. "No, Georgie, Dadda's not coming home ever again. It's just you and me now, love."

Rose shifted the weight of her meagre bundle and turned on her heel, walking briskly into an unknown future. A future without Ralph, without a home, and without a job, but she still had her Georgie, and she would die before she would lose him.

# *First Love*

## PETER CORRIN

Forty-three years on, and still the spell
Draws me back to this place we knew so well.
Where, essence now, two youngsters love and laugh
And haunt the fields and wander sunny paths,
Where still the crows call raucously from trees
And myriad buds and bugs rejoice in summer's breeze.
Where magick and laughter hang unmoved, like wraiths,
Secured by memories shared in this unmoving place.
Where even now I can recall your happiness,
Your spirit calls out yet to my still emptiness.
And love, unfinished, like a cut-short song,
Pervades the air and will so long
As we both breathe. Do you still think
Of those long days when we would drink
From our cup of love and dream great hopes,
Hand in hand upon those green sward slopes?
Have you forgotten all that we held dear?
Those views, those woods, the waters clear,
The kisses snatched, the joy we wove,
That first bright cherished breath of love?
And have you let slip all we shared when young,
Those years ago, when we left our song unsung?

# Barney Bites the Dust

### JENNY MURPHY

Friday is my day for a lie-in, hopefully. Not this Friday as the phone and the dog competed for my attention at seven in the morning. My doggy-walking friend had been sad all week as one of her dogs was in doggy intensive care. She had spent a considerable amount of time doggy visiting, but all to no avail. Barney was dead. I tried to imagine my life without my dog Charlie and could not, so I asked if I could do anything. She sadly told me that there was nothing to do as the hole was dug in her front garden and that was it.

By the time I had showered, dressed, and answered a few more calls, she was on my doorstep. Apparently, my knowledge of funerals was required. She pointed to Barney, who was on the front seat of her car looking decidedly dead. My dog-walking friend wondered if my dog Charlie might want a chance to pay his last respects. This presented a slight problem as behaviour and social graces are not his strong points. He was more likely to seize his opportunity to leap lustfully onto the deceased than to shed a doggy tear.

I hastily refused the offer and suggested that I follow her home to assist with the doggy funeral, using my own car to allow for a hasty retreat, and to avoid the possibility of having to share a seat with a dead dog.

Pulling up outside her house, I found my instincts had been correct. Barney was not heading swiftly for the handy hole but for the house. Lagging behind, I almost fell over Barney and his mistress, who were now prostrated in the entrance hall. Her other two dogs were dutifully sniffing the departed, and I breathed a sigh of relief for the absence of my dog Charlie.

Barney, now wrapped in his favourite blanket and with his favourite squeaky toy under his chin, was being greatly admired. I felt it only correct to join in, so I gave him a stroke, admired his weight and coat, and felt drawn to remark that his passing must have been peaceful as his legs seemed in a natural pose and he did not have a startled look, but rather a healthy glow on his face.

The vet did not uphold my dead dog diagnostic view, but I did not feel the need to argue the point as the end result was the same. There was a definite chill, not to mention whiff, in the air. Barney was cold, stiff, and most definitely dead.

Saved by the doorbell and the appearance of an ex-husband dutifully weeping, I declared myself surplus to requirements and skipped off.

Possibly, I am only good at funerals for people.

*COMMENDED in the 2014*
*Somerset Short Story Competition*

# *Imagination Reconciled*

## FAITH MOULIN

Mary-Ann Lindeman was a tortured soul. Sorrow was etched in her face. A tear was forming in her eye, time was etching deep lines in her forehead and her cheeks were losing their former plumpness to a stony pallor, pitted with dark blemishes. Peter looked at her with a sadness as heavy as a fattened hog. "I love you," he whispered.

He liked being in this calm place with her. He didn't find it spooky, or eerie, like some people did. He found it soothing, peaceful. He liked the paucity of people and the way that those who did come here kept themselves to themselves, each embracing their own grief, hugging it to themselves, keeping it as close as a snared rabbit that must not be allowed to escape. Wild birds sang in the old trees and now and again the squirrels chased each other with an energy that seemed out of place, but Peter sat so quietly on the kerbstone that wild creatures didn't even notice him.

Peter Lindeman was nine years old, a boy with a love of magic and mystery. His mother said his head was in the clouds. She often said she didn't want anyone else in her life whose head was full of nonsense. She had become very bitter since Peter's father had left, taking his anthology of ghost stories and their neighbour Bethan with him. They now lived in London, and he had become quite rich and famous, but she still said his books were rubbish.

Peter studied the inscription:

*Mary-Ann Lindeman*
*Beloved wife of Richard Lindeman*
*Alderman of this town*

*"A faithful wife"*
*Taken from us in her 22nd year*
*6 August 1897*

Peter's father had told him the tragic story. Mary-Ann had been
engaged to be married to a local lad she had known all her life. He was
apprenticed to a carpenter. It took seven years to become qualified and
the young lovers had longed for the apprenticeship to be over so they
could marry. Once he was twenty-one he would be earning enough
money to support a wife and, in time, a family. They would rent a
cottage and she would work at home, making hats for the milliner and
looking after their babies, while he would be a journeyman, paid by
the day for his skill with wood. Mary-Ann was looking forward to
making curtains and bedcovers and a rag rug for their hearth. She
would sit by the fire on a chair made by her handsome young husband,
and in the evenings when the children were in bed, he would be
chiselling, sanding and waxing a swinging cradle, a dolly's bed or a
footstool.

Then came tragedy. Typhoid struck as quickly as a fox in the
henhouse. Mary-Ann's father, mother, two sisters and a brother all
died, along with hundreds of others. Trade was brisk at the carpenter's
shop and the workbench was never silent as the daily demand for
coffins blunted their saw teeth and their strength. After three weeks the
old carpenter himself gave up his awl and died. The apprenticeship
was over.

Richard Lindeman, merchant, alderman and a twice-widowed, self-
styled full-blooded man, set his heart on the young and beautiful
orphan, Mary-Ann. He wooed her, fed her and dressed her in silk. He
begged, implored, bribed and wrestled with her reluctance until at last
she married him, but, in the way of Victorian romances, she was never
happy because she longed for her young carpenter. She also longed for
a child, but she hated the process by which she could gain one from
the alderman. Her husband had robbed her of her youth, her life and
her love, and she could not return his affection and yield to him. For

his part he was tired of her refusals and procrastination and he felt justified in taking that which Mary-Ann would not give.

Mary-Ann died in childbirth just under a year after their wedding. Richard Lindeman was philosophical: "These things happen," he said, and he showed his grief to the world through the adornment of her grave with a life-size angel.

Peter's mother had said that the marble figure wasn't really her: it was just a representation in stone. It was just a statue of an angel; it wasn't meant to be Mary-Ann at all. But Peter knew that his mother didn't know everything. She sometimes even admitted it when he tired her out with a catalogue of curiosity and asked too many questions. She would sigh, "I don't know everything, Peter." Sometimes she added with spite, "Not like your father."

Every time Peter saw Mary-Ann she was changing. The changes were subtle and gradual, but he knew without the sanction of science that the angel's sad face had become Mary-Ann's sad face, entrenched with her sorrow and patched with lichen, little medallions of grey, green and orange encrusting her skin over the decades. She looked at him with longing. He knew she loved him. He was beginning to love her too.

Other Lindemans were all around them. Some had marble urns, some had big grey stones with arched tops, and one, James Lindeman, aged fifty-two, lay under a cross made of granite speckled like a baby blackbird's breast, made in 1894. This was Peter's favourite place, among the Lindemans, where he belonged. His father would be buried here when he died; he had said so. Peter's mother was suddenly angry that afternoon and said he was a stupid man to burden his child with a statement like that, but Peter didn't find that too hard to bear. What was hard to bear was his mother's constant rage and his father's constant absence.

He looked up at Mary-Ann again. She was looking down on him, not with a hard stare, in spite of her blank stone eyes, but with a look as tender as spring tears. If his heart had been stone it would have melted.

And it was melting. His very flesh was melting. His soft, smooth, warm, young skin had become slack and was liquefying; he was flowing to her through the earth, losing consciousness, losing shape. Mary-Ann comforted him with an earthy embrace, the dampness of her tears warm and cleansing. This was love and peace: a peace not as the world gives.

Peter's mother was frantic but furious. He was old enough not to go wandering off scaring her to death. His father was, of course, as usual, out of it. He was in London, not having to deal with his stupid boy whose head he had filled with silly nonsense. The police were useless too. They sent divers into the canal and lake and searched the woods but they could find no trace of Peter. An old lady who had seen a boy hanging around in the churchyard gave a description that matched Peter's, but they didn't find him. He had disappeared.

"Who put that there?" said the monumental mason a couple of weeks later. He was upset to find a beautiful sculpture had arrived in his domain overnight without notice. "I do all the memorial stones around here," he said to anyone who would listen. "Where did that one come from?" Next to Mary-Ann Lindeman was a new cherub – a cheeky, fat-faced, limestone cherub, his chubby legs bare and chill, heavy against the plinth. The mason bent down to look for his rival's mark.

"It's beautifully done," said an old woman kneeling nearby while she arranged flowers in a jam jar for her husband's grave. She had always felt inferior, conscious that some people might see the more extravagant Lindeman monuments and think her mean. Her husband had a plain, but tasteful, rectangle of Cornish slate, sparingly carved and smooth as beech bark.

The mason had to nod his agreement. The carving on the stone cherub was out of this world. "God knows where it came from," he said. "It's got no maker's mark." As he got to his feet he glanced at the other Lindeman memorials. "That angel's got a beautiful smile," he said in awe. He had never even noticed it before.

# The Offer

## GUY JENKINSON

"It's really very simple," said the Emissary to the President. "You merely have to choose between unconditional compliance... and immediate replacement."

The World President turned away from his visitor to look out of the window. From his penthouse office on the two-hundredth floor of the Global Administration Tower his view ranged over ninety kilometres, from the metropolis bustling unseen far below to the glowering sunset disappearing into the ocean on the misty horizon.

He turned to face the Emissary again. "Replacement?" he queried, stiffly.

"*Your* replacement," replied the Emissary evenly, "then – if necessary – that of your successor, then his successor and so on... until someone co-operates, and agrees to our terms. It's very civilised, and far more cost-effective than the use of military force."

He gestured with a gloved, three-clawed hand and a small ceramic triangle, inscribed with a glowing insignia, materialised from nowhere to drop onto the President's desk.

"I am empowered to negotiate and to procure as an accredited representative of the Interstellar Mercantile Conglomerate," he said, formally. He spoke quietly, his cultured tones conveying word-perfect Standard English, although his voice seemed to emanate from a strange, many-faceted crystal carried on a burnished metal armband.

The President found the Emissary's sheer presence unnerving. Although humanoid, his species had obviously evolved originally from reptiles, just as humans descended from primates. A bipedal, tail-less lizard with a scaly, grey-green skin, the alien exceeded two metres in height.

By human standards, he was quite heavily built; his unblinking eyes gleamed like polished marble. Loosely swathed in a metallic silver toga, his image shimmered disturbingly – slightly out of focus – as if an energy-field surrounded him.

"I understand," said the President, his face grim as he tried to mask his instinctive fear and distaste. He had no doubt that the threatened "replacements" could indeed be implemented, and that no power on Earth could prevent that from happening.

A few hours earlier, dozens of immense spacecraft had appeared in synchronous orbit around the Earth. Within a single microsecond, the entire fleet had flashed into existence from previously empty space. Later, the featureless spheres had descended to hover silently in the stratosphere, ignoring all attempts at communication. Any craft approaching them were simply turned away by a gentle but irresistible force that seemed to bend space back upon itself.

Like the ships, the Emissary had also appeared without warning: materialising in the President's office, apparently out of thin air. Ominously, every communication device in the building – including the President's direct link to Security – had failed at exactly that instant.

The alien vessels had not been threatened or attacked: it was obvious to Earth's military commanders that it would be pointless to confront such awesome technology with force. Earth's defenders had also discovered that the aliens were detectable only in the visible-light part of the electromagnetic spectrum; at all other wavelengths, they simply did not exist.

Under his breath, the President mused, *"Any sufficiently advanced technology seems like magic."* Aloud, he admitted, "I guess you can impose upon us whatever conditions you wish." Once more looking into the sunset, he contemplated the elongated shadow cast by a distant alien ship. "That much is obvious! Your forces are overwhelming, to say the least." Despite a dry mouth his voice remained firm.

Fighting to overcome his apprehension, the President continued,

"I'm not particularly concerned about my own fate, but I *am* responsible for the people of my world – and not just the forty-six percent who voted for me!" He studied the Emissary's leathery features, but the impassive alien displayed no reaction to the human's ancient political joke. *I see, no sense of humour*, thought the President, as he returned to his desk. *Still, what did I expect? All I can do now is sit down, concentrate on retaining my sanity, listen to this... whatever it is – and pray.*

Leaning back in his armchair, the President closed his eyes and willed his body to relax. Controlling his breathing, he cleared his mind and concentrated on marshalling his skills and experience to face the most critical diplomatic event in Earth's history. Gradually, his thumping pulse slowed. For a moment, he gazed at the portraits of his six predecessors, fixed to the wall opposite his desk. *Wish me luck, people*, he thought. *Let's open the scoring.*

His outward composure regained – and a little surprised at his own calmness – he forced himself to make eye contact with the Emissary, demanding, "Very well – tell me, just what does compliance mean? Bottom line: what's in it for us humans?" His voice hardened as he asked defiantly, "And why unconditional?"

Without waiting for an answer he hurried on, "As a race, we value freedom. This may sound futile, but we *will* resist oppression!" He stopped, suddenly realising that his nerves had let his tongue outrun his brain. *Keep calm, you fool – keep calm!*

Had he been human, the Emissary would have raised an eyebrow; as it was, he slowly blinked the nictitating membrane down over each eyeball in turn – an equivalent gesture for his species.

"Oppression? Absolutely not!" The alien shook his head vigorously in denial.

He explained: "Compliance just means joining the IMC, thus placing your planet under its protection." Folding his bulky frame into the chair facing the President's desk, he continued, "And unconditional simply means accepting overall IMC sovereignty in your off-world affairs... that's all."

He went on, "Let me justify our position, and forgive my pointing out that we have enjoyed many more years of cultural development than you – a few centuries more, by our reckoning." The Emissary paused, looking directly at the President, who made no reply but gestured politely that his visitor should continue.

"For three hundred years, your planet has endured poverty, famines, pandemics, slavery, wars, pollution and self-inflicted ecological disasters... on a global scale. Your most recent conflict was biochemical, when you barely avoided a full-scale thermonuclear exchange!"

Surprised at his visitor's knowledge of Earth's history, the President remained silent as the alien continued, "By way of comparison, the Conglomerate has suffered no major disruption or conflict of any kind since its founding, a millennium ago. Free from violence and pollution, it has prospered, whereas you attained planetary unity only five decades ago—"

"We avoided extinction!" interrupted the President, nettled by the alien's frank – and unexpected – indictment. Calculating rapidly, he added, "During the first one hundred and fifty years of our so-called Atomic Era, nuclear weapons have been used only six times—"

"So few times!" scoffed the alien, "yet the aftermath of those events is still evident, over seventy years later. History records the slaughter of some five hundred million humans."

Relentlessly, the Emissary warmed to his subject. "Despite unification, you still experience rampant crime, widespread terrorism, petty sectarian conflicts, vicious tribal squabbles and – as always – overpopulation. Dozens of your provincial cities are nothing but breeding sites. Every year, over one hundred million additional humans are born into hopeless poverty."

He leaned forward, accusingly. "Humans are by far the most prolific breeders on the planet, yet some of your food-animals are treated better than many of your own kind. Billions of humans exist in conditions that are more 'battery' than 'free-range'."

Fleetingly, the President wondered if the alien's comment had been a laboured attempt at humour. Resenting being lectured, he responded to the alien's final point, "It could have been worse. After all, we have half the population predicted a century ago *and* we've moderated its rate of increase. We *learn* from our mistakes... and we continue to do so!"

"Quite so," agreed the Emissary. "The planet now supports only eleven billion humans whose numbers will take an entire seventy-seven years to double." This last remark was delivered in the same urbane, neutral voice as the rest of his conversation and, to human ears at least, seemed wholly devoid of irony.

"I'm very impressed," observed the President, politely. Inwardly, his thoughts seethed, *What the hell is this leading to? So far, I've been threatened, propositioned, lectured and reprimanded for all of mankind's failings back to the last century and beyond! What the blazes does this "Emissary" actually* want? Aloud he remarked, "You appear to be exceedingly well-informed about us."

"Indeed," replied the Emissary. "When I was called in by IMC Audit it had been some centuries since Survey had visited this planet, so Development insisted that we spend time observing you – covertly, of course – before making this first contact."

Pausing to think of a suitable comparison, he continued, "Recall from your own history the disastrous impact of the Spanish on South America, some six centuries ago."

The President nodded. "I am familiar with the culture clash between sixteenth-century Spanish explorers and the indigenous races: the Aztecs, Mayas, Incas and so on. Are we that far behind you, comparatively speaking?"

The Emissary seemed almost apologetic. "Much farther behind. Perhaps the case of the Australian aborigines versus the nineteenth-century British is more appropriate." He shrugged. "I'm sorry if that example bruises your ego. However, we always avoid such discord... now. We long ago learned from our expensive mistakes! We would never try to impose our beliefs or value-systems on you. As part of 'first-contact protocol', we control our interaction so that exposure to superior technology does not destroy native cultures."

As an afterthought he added, "Nor would we accidentally inflict upon you our diseases, against which you could have no natural immunity... again, look to your own history!"

Concluding that humankind's record was probably indefensible, and wishing rather to change the subject, the President conceded, "Very well, you've made your point about our dismal record. At this moment, I'm not sure that I see a clear direction in our discussion. Perhaps we can move on? What does membership of this Conglomerate actually entail?"

The Emissary's expression registered the reptilian equivalent of a smile, a mirthless display of serrated teeth that did nothing to reassure his human counterpart.

"Not as much as you might imagine," he replied, "because it is an organisation primarily dedicated to commerce. As long as you accept membership of the IMC, obey its rules and accede to our overall control in all matters of external policy, then – internally – you will remain a self-governing entity.

"Speaking of the rules," – he gestured, and a metre-high stack of data crystals shimmered into reality on the President's desk – "that's the abridged version. It contains a new members' introductory pack," he added, helpfully. He paused, whilst the President silently regarded his freshly loaded desktop with a jaundiced eye.

"We encompass a multitude of races in the Conglomerate; indeed, we pride ourselves on its multi-species basis, taking harmony for granted. As long as planetary governments work peacefully within IMC rules, we rarely intervene in anyone's internal affairs."

The alien leaned back in his armchair. "Furthermore, as a member of the IMC you are both entitled and required to send a representative to sit on the Board."

"The Board?" asked the President, warily.

"Its full name is the Interstellar Mercantile Conglomerate Affiliate Members' Board (Administration & Policy) – IMCAMBAP, for short," explained the Emissary. "Every IMC member world is represented there. I believe you would call that democracy."

*I would call it bureaucracy*, thought the President. *We seem to have that much in common.*

The Emissary waited, silent, immobile as a statue whilst the President sank back into his chair, lost in thought for several minutes. Eventually, he sat up straight and addressed the alien: "It sounds very... interesting out there; peaceful and harmonious, you said?"

The Emissary nodded. "From a purely political-military viewpoint it is but, commercially, our well-ordered galaxy does enjoy some robust trading. Consider it an acceptable substitute for conflict, or a safe outlet for the pressures that used to result in conflict. Adherents to your creed of capitalism should feel quite at home in the Conglomerate."

"I'm sure they will," said the President, beginning to feel slightly more at ease, "but I'm still concerned about another, rather basic issue. Your offer is interesting, but what could we trade? Our technology is centuries behind yours and our natural resources are already over-stretched coping with our own global economy." Unable to resist the jibe, he added, "I can't imagine what services we might offer; are you proposing that we peddle artefacts of our primitive culture to sophisticated IMC tourists?

"*Like beggars in a backwater province*," he muttered under his breath.

"Not at all," countered the Emissary smoothly. "As far as interstellar commerce is concerned, IMC members deal in any item or service that sells. Nothing is forbidden and the regulations refer mostly to fair dealing. In your case, the one asset that you have is agrarian. Specifically, we can see you as a potential exporter of consumable animal tissue."

At this, the President felt a sudden lessening of tension; what had started as an invasion nightmare had become trade negotiation... even though, as he reminded himself, it was being imposed at the metaphorical point of a gun. A wave of relief flooded his soul.

"You mean *meat*?" he asked, some of his confidence returning.

"Correct," replied the Emissary. "According to our provisional assessment, this planet should be able to sustain an export of over one hundred million carcasses per year."

"I'm no expert on the meat trade," said the President, "but I can soon have some of our experts in the Global Resources Office confirm your figures. What types of meat are you likely to require – cows, sheep, pigs, goats... poultry... even sea-mammals, perhaps?"

There was a long pause, then the Emissary stood up from his chair and towered over the human behind the desk. "Obviously, I didn't make myself completely clear," he said, coldly. "You manage the population sizes of your lesser food-animals satisfactorily. I was actually referring to the one hundred million additional *humans* that you over-produce so effortlessly each year and who have no future except to consume, breed and pollute!"

Stunned into silence, unable to believe what he had just heard, the President finally understood – too late – the truly *alien* nature of his visitor. The glib façade of urbane discussion vanished in an instant and his spirit collapsed into an abyss of despair.

Indifferent to the President's reaction, the Emissary continued relentlessly, "Their export will be a relief to your economy and, if necessary, the IMC Produce Intervention Commission will take them off your hands. You may be surprised at the demand in the Conglomerate for pre-packaged primate. Warm-blood produce always sells well, and any surplus meat is absorbed by the various pet-food industries." With a dismissive gesture, he added, "After all, you don't produce anything else of value in sufficient quantities to interest the IMC."

Shocked into paralysis by the horrific implications of the alien's words, the President remained unresponsive. Open-mouthed, he stared blankly at the impassive Emissary, who continued, "Considering your mismanagement so far, you have no other viable options. Before too long, pollution will render this world unfit for any kind of commerce... and we will not allow that kind of waste to occur!" He snorted. "Anyway, such a situation is forbidden, under IMC rules."

The President leapt to his feet, desperate to respond effectively.

Wild-eyed, he screamed at the alien, "This is monstrous!"

Struggling to find an appropriate protest, all he could deliver was a pathetic: "This is completely unacceptable – it's totally unethical!"

"Unethical?" snapped the Emissary. "Ethics have nothing to do with it; this is *business*, and we're making an offer you cannot refuse! In any case, if things proceed unchanged you'll soon need that surplus meat yourselves... to feed the rest."

# The Legend of
# El Cid and the Leper

### VICTORIA HELEN TURNER

Rodrigo Diaz of Bivar,
Immortal hero of Spain,
Whom history called El Cid – the Lord –
Set out one day with his knights,
On pilgrimage to Compostella.

His great white war horse shone
In blinding silver light in the
White-hot gold of the Spanish sun.
The sun's heat had not yet scorched the earth,
And great storms had caused oozing mud and mires
By the roadside.

The Cid heard
A pitiful cry for help
Mingling with the beat of horses' hooves
And jingling harness.
He halted his men, dismounted,
And walked quickly in the direction
Of the cry.

A little way from the road
He saw one of the filthy mires and
In it up to his waist,
Being sucked greedily down
By the ravenous monster of vile mud,
Was an old man – raising his arms in terror,
Crying,
'Help me – for the love of God!'

Rodrigo called to his men for help,
But the knights drew back in fear.
'My Lord,' they shouted,
'Let him die – he is a leper!'

The Cid looked at them with disgust –
'The hearts of those of you who call yourselves Christians
Are more foul than this man's disease!' and
He strode into the mire, grabbed the man's shoulders
And heaved him out by himself,
Whilst his brave warriors cowered and looked on!

He lifted the old man onto his horse
And took him to the nearest inn where
They were to lodge for the night.
His men, crossing themselves,
Went to the farthest part of the room.
But Rodrigo, who had given a clean robe to the leper,
Shared food with him from the same dish,
As no one would come near them.
He shared the same rough bed
In a small chamber.

At midnight,
When Rodrigo was fast asleep,
The leper turned towards him
And breathed through Rodrigo's shoulders
And so strong was it that
It passed through to his breast and he
Awoke in fear –
The leper had disappeared,
But a bright light filled the room.
He sat up and a being in a white raiment
Stood before him,
Shining with the bright light.

'Fear not, Rodrigo of Bivar, called El Cid.
I am Saint Lazarus – and I was
That leper whom you helped
For the love of God,
And because you did this for His sake,
God has granted you a great gift,
And that breath which has passed through you,
From me, is a little of the Divine Breath,
And because you only do honourable deeds
And only for good
So God has honoured you,
And his breath will make you
Invincible to all those who are evil,
Whom you will destroy for the sake
Of goodness and justice and in His name.
When your time comes,
You will have achieved your great destiny,
And will die naturally and with honour
And be immortal in the minds of good men – forever!
For God hath blessed thee!' – and he disappeared.

Rodrigo fell onto his knees,
Thanking and praising God.
So it came to pass –
In God's name he saved Spain
From an evil enemy,
And saved the people of Spain –
Christian and Moor alike –
And rode into history
As the noblest and purest knight of Spain –
And most of all – of God!

# *Pirate's Homecomin'*

### PETER CORRIN

A boy stood on the burning deck, thank Heaven 'twas not this ship,
We've had enough of troubles, though, to blight us on this trip.

We'm sailing home to Brissle fair from out there on the Main,
The weather has been more than foul for summer months off Spain.

But now we'm on the homeward league, this bit is all downhill,
I'm sure I smell the old King's Arms and over yonder's Pill.

We found a coupla Spanish tubs all laden down with gold.
We sent them to the bottom, lads; their gold is in *our* hold!

We had to have our bottom scraped whilst we was in Jamaicy
It's not as painful as it sounds and super quick it make 'ee!

The crew have all been seasick, mate, at least those that survived
That plague just out of Kingston. Then somehow we contriv'd

To leave another fourteen crew on some Karibbyan isle
When the Navy – uninvited – sneaked up on us in style.

We lost our Jolly Roger flag – a lucky Navy shot.
The other one that hit us, mate, blew t'rudder all to pot!

And then there was the mutiny, 'bout carryin' these ladies.
Me pistol and me cutlass sent them thar dogs to Hades!

The cook, he died – somethin' he ate? I wooden doubt it, babber.
A pusser ship-born cook he was – a vast behind and flabber!

'Tis always sad to lose some crew, this time 'twas nigh on forty,
It makes this scow a pig to sail but helps when sharin' booty!

We'm spent a bit and hid a bit and brought the rest home wi' us,
We may still look quite raggedy but we are pirates fierce!

So, here we be, back home again. The ship will need some mending,
But you shipyard can deal wi' that; our doubloons we'll be spending!

One of the great advantages of losing crew, yer see,
Is that there's more gold left, me dears, fer lookin' after me!

# A Royal Wedding in Somerset

### BRIAN HUMPHREYS

William sat on the throne, trying to remember details of his night out with Harry. His fiancée Kate shouted up the stairs, 'Breakfast is on the table.' She knew that William hated it when she shouted up the stairs.

After a late-night session with his brother, breakfast for William was usually two choices: take it or leave it, but this morning, his fiancée had made a special effort. He came downstairs to find a full English breakfast of bacon, sausages, mushrooms, eggs and tomatoes, with fried bread on the side. He absently scratched his crown jewels and yawned. 'Morning, Kate; breakfast looks fit for a king.'

Sitting down to her customary two boiled eggs, a slim-line Kate avoided eye contact. 'Morning, Willie.' She always called him 'Willie' when he was in her bad books, and William was fully aware of this.

'"Morning Willie" is how someone might address their manhood first thing in the morning, hardly the correct way to address a member of the Royal family.'

'Excuse me, your majesty, but who died and made you king? There's no need to get above your station.' The use of clichés and puns was deliberate because William hated them.

'I don't get above my station – do I?'

'No, your majesty,' replied Kate, smashing the shell of an egg with her spoon. 'So what did you and Harry get up to last night? Come on, spill the beans.' She decided to squeeze in as many clichés as she could.

Beans! William knew there was something wrong with breakfast. No baked beans. *What's going on?* He had tomatoes instead of beans.

*Does she think I'm getting fat?* He ate another mouthful of food. 'Kate, do you think I'm getting fat?'

Kate looked him over. 'You know what they say; a minute on the lips, a lifetime on the hips. It wouldn't hurt you to get into shape for the wedding photographs.' That would teach him for staying out late with his brother.

'I'm round. That's a shape, isn't it? It's not like I haven't tried to lose weight; it's just that one's body and one's fat have become real good friends.'

Kate cracked her second boiled egg as if to say, *this is what you should be eating – healthy food, not fried bacon and sausage,* then she asked again about last night. 'Did you go clubbing?'

A silly grin spread across William's face. 'Don't be silly, Kate, there are no seals in Weston-super-Mare.'

Kate ignored him. He was always childish after a night out with Harry. 'He never takes life seriously, does he?'

'Who, the laughing policeman?'

'You know full well who I mean: your brother Harry. He gets right up my nose.'

'That reminds me of one of Harry's jokes: "Why do gorillas have big nostrils?"' He could see from the look on her face that she would not answer, so in a poor attempt at a female voice, he answered his own question. '"I don't know, Harry; why do gorillas have big nostrils?" "Because they have big fingers!"' William laughed aloud at his joke-telling skills.

Seeing that Kate was not impressed, William tried to be serious.

'Last night, Harry suggested that we should both return to Africa to give more support to that AIDS charity we helped a few years ago.'

'Is that before our wedding, or afterwards?'

'Kate, will you please go easy on Harry? After our marriage he will be left all on his own, and right now, he just doesn't know who he is any more. He feels a bit like that guy from Wham! when George Michael left.'

'What guy?'

'Exactly!'

Kate steered the conversation towards wedding matters. 'William, we still have important decisions to make; for instance, what will you do with your corgis once we are married?'

William was straight on the defensive. 'I'm not getting rid of them; they have brought me untold pleasure for many years.'

'Can't Harry look after them for you?'

'You must be joking. Harry can't look after himself, never mind my corgis. They need care and attention. I'll have you know, some of them are nearly forty years old.'

'And they look it too,' sighed Kate. On more than one occasion, she had sat on one left on the settee, or found one in their bed.

William removed one of his corgis from his trouser pocket. 'I admit that some of my corgis do need a lick of paint, like this light blue miniature Ford Anglia police car.' He held it before his eyes, studying it like a jeweller assessing an exquisite diamond.

'Little things please little minds,' said Kate, wishing that he would see her as an object of desire. She felt better for getting the Corgi problem out in the open. All's fair in love and war. *Goodness,* she thought, *I'm even thinking in clichés now.*

William decided to divert the conversation *back* to the wedding, a grave misjudgement. 'I thought you were happy with our fairytale royal wedding in Somerset? The abbey is booked, and many girls dream of walking down the aisle in an abbey.'

'Ah, yes, the ruins of Glastonbury Abbey: every young girl's dream wedding venue.'

'Well, it may not be too late to book Weston-super-Mare Grand Pier. Do you want me to phone them?'

'Oh, be still my beating heart! Weston's Grand Pier, every young girl's second dream wedding venue.'

'And don't forget, I've booked the castle for the evening reception.'

'Ah yes, the castle at Banwell, and we all know what parking is like at Banwell Castle. These wedding arrangements are hardly the red carpet treatment, are they? William, it's as plain as the nose on your face, we are not singing from the same hymn sheet.'

Much to Kate's annoyance, William took another Corgi out of his pocket, and began to use sound effects as he moved the two of them around the kitchen table, replicating a car chase. 'Brrrrrumm, yeeeeooooow, da da da da,' he sang, weaving the cars between the salt and pepper containers.

That was the straw that broke the camel's back. He was asking for it, and come hell or high water, he was going to get it, right between the eyes. She took a deep breath and decided to hit him with both barrels; after all, you always hurt the one you love.

'William, I know you think that you are a diamond geezer, but at the end of the day, with all due respect, when all is said and done, we have to face the facts, *Willie*.'

She put so much emphasis on the word 'Willie', William stopped the car chase and looked up.

'There's no point in beating around the bush; I can safely say, without fear of contradiction, that you are all icing and no cake. In fact, the only thing regal about you, William Royal – is your surname!'

# *Found*

## BARBARA EVANS

On the fuzzy ground the glittering necklace of the tiny stream lies coiled and twisted amongst the grassy tussocks; now seen, now unseen. Dark its bed when you can see it. A rich golden tan, and there are rocks here and there, white-grey, topped with vivid emerald moss. The air is cool and sharp and the sky is high and blue, endless blue. Ellen has come to the top of the slope.

The back of the cottage garden rises up to meet the lowest shoulder of the mountain and she comes here often. It is close by; close enough to be able to take a short break away from the house and go and walk in the crystal air. A call from the front door will easily bring her back down, and it is close enough to the kitchen if there is bread that is proving or a pie baking.

She has just clambered over the low wicket fence. It is just a parched, pale-blue painted wooden fence. It is hardly as high as her hip, so it is easy to hoist her skirts and step over.

Her strides are long and cover the ground rapidly. They send her skirts swirling around her as she goes higher and higher. She loves the swishing feel of it. Her skirts *should* be in motion, full of life. She herself wants to be in constant motion, all of the time, all of her days, and most of all she loves walking on the mountain.

When she is doing her chores, or just going about the house, her gowns hang upon her like heavy tapestries, they have none of the life that she has now instilled in them by her easy, wind-borne, life-filled gait.

Her head is up and she is sucking the electric air into her body. It seems like food to her. Life-increasing, life-nourishing, perfumed air. There is a breath of lake water in it, mixed with heather, and there is a tinge of odour from the sheep on the high paths. The stream smells metallic, and meadow flowers and the bruised grass beneath her feet supply their familiar accents.

To be outside is simply lovely! It is now that she feels truly alive and part of nature. On the mountain she can become a daughter of Eve and enter Eden. It is now that she can put aside everything else. For the duration of the walk, only Ellen herself exists, there is only herself in the here and now of the time and place. It is her place, she is safe here. That is the joy of it.

The bluebird sky swoops down upon her as she lies out on the tussocky couch and gazes upwards. All of this is reduced to the compass of her sight and only the clouds exist. There are only the vague shapes and colours of her peripheral vision encompassing the whole, like a frame.

She will not be able to linger long. The warmth and duties of the kitchen are calling her and it really is not quite warm enough to sit about. Why didn't she bring her shawl?

There is a stone sticking awkwardly into her shoulder blade and she shifts slightly, but cannot find any better spot. The grass prickles her face and the thicker stems press spikes into the back of her neck. A wild cold gust of breeze disturbs her skirts and whips her hair into a frenzy. She has become aware of the pastry under her fingernails and the marks on her apron. She is not really fit to be seen out and about; how she wishes that she had tied on a new fresh apron before she set off.

Suddenly the sun is blotted out!

A huge shadow has fallen across her gaze, and a shriek of fear leaves her lips. The shadow has cloaked her so completely and so suddenly that she reacts instinctively. Is it some sort of attack? The shadow passes in a flash but it proves to be not far from the truth, for a giant bird certainly took her to be some sort of carrion. Now it has swerved away again; it has found that she is no such thing. There must be a dead sheep nearby, a still-born lamb or else an afterbirth. She notices several birds in the air; some are crows, the hoodies, and the really large crows must be ravens! The eagle that frightened her and its mate have alighted on some boulders nearby.

Struggling to her feet, she refits her boots. Her eye drifts down the dell, curious about the cause of the birds' interest. There is something threaded through the tussocky, lumpy, rocky slope. A figure, a female figure, half-absorbed into the hillside, can be seen. Her hips, her hands and her head can be seen only in parts. Grass and boulders hide her and the spaces between reveal her.

It is plain that she must have lain there the whole night through, and it seems certain therefore that she must have already given up her life and she breathes no more. Her figure lies spread out, relaxed into her final rest; her hair like a halo of black flame is spread about her on the heather, framing her face like a queen of the night. Pale and luminous like the moon she lies, with an extra beauty bequeathed to her by the bloodless hand of death. Only the faint blue spreading through her lips betrays the cause of her spirit-like complexion.

Sticky red marks smudge her body and her clothes. A smear runs across one cheek and she has red painted on both arms. There is no pulse in her wrist and no life throbs a signal from the big vein in her neck. The folds of her dress, the fabric of her dark blue skirts are pulled and piled over her thighs, forming a soft hummock. Her hands lie across her abdomen, each preventing the other from falling to her side. It seems that they cup the mound of bunched-up clothing.

Underneath something stirs. There is a child! A new-born infant is cradled and cupped in her lap. It still has the cord attached, and the dress covers it against the cold. So cold is the child that only a little life lingers in its tiny face.

Ellen pulls the child from its nest and clutches it to her bosom, and she tears open her bodice to bring it nearer to her heart. Urgently she rips a sharp stone through the cord to release the infant from its mother. There are no wrappings, no shawl that she can use to cover the dead beauty's face, and she has nothing to cover the child from the chill either. Instead she cups its curled-up vulnerability with her straw bonnet. The infant starts to whimper feebly in her embrace.

As she turns to go, she reaches out and touches the dead damsel's face, for she is full of pity at the loss of such a young and beautiful girl, then she returns with her tiny burden back down the hill. This child needs the warmth of her bread-baked kitchen.

She sends one of the street-boys down to the minister's house with a message, and he and the sextant come up with some men to take the poor corpse away from the mountain. They carry her down on a board, her pale face and fine nose pointed at the deeply dark, grey-blue sky. Her long black hair flows over the end of the board, sweeping the men's hands and sometimes their faces. Ellen leaves the child warm and sleeping and runs out to see her come down. All around doors open and people step out of their cottages to see the spectacle. It seems like a royal funeral bier that passes, a royal procession. The poor maiden seems like a princess or a queen, of faeries or men: who could tell?

Just then rain comes, and drops of heavenly tears splash spots onto the maiden's gown and shine her face. The rain increases to a downpour as she enters the village, cleansing her poor body of the birth blood, washing away the work of childbirth.

Two days later Ellen takes the baby to the graveside, holding her close. The child must be her chief mourner, though she knows it not. She stands with the babe by the grave as the lady is buried. There are only a few people there to mourn her, just the minister, the matrons of the village and the men who carried her down.

Ellen tumbles a handful of soil into the grave, and a posy of wildflowers that she has caused the child to clutch and hold. Standing there she leans and whispers a pledge to the mysterious woman.

"Dear damsel," she says, "I have named your child 'Meredith', and I will keep her from harm."

Years have passed, but no one has ever come to the village to ask for news of the beautiful lost lady. All enquiries have yielded nothing. I doubt that anyone of her kin knows that there was a child born.

Ellen thinks herself so very blessed, to have been given such a child to care for. Meredith has been sunshine and showers, and fresh-scented blossom. All the beauties and promise of spring seem to be embodied in her nature. The two women have become inseparable.

Ellen has grown into matronly maturity and Meredith into her natural beauty. She has grown strong and tall, with black hair down to her waist. She is a mirror of her mother, and in her full blossoming, she has heard and understood God's call to nature. The call to find a companion for life.

Yes, she did look for a young man to stand by her and give her a home and family. Yes, she did fall in love, more than once, but she has never yet settled for anyone. Instead, Ellen and Meredith have happily lived together, in the cosy cot at the foot of the mountain.

# FIFTY-WORD STORIES

### FAITH MOULIN

## Boys Will Be Boys

A century ago brave boys, only fourteen, signed up to be soldiers. They fought, some died; their age was of no account. They took responsibility.

Now suave men, over forty, strive to be boys. They have their PlayStations and teenage lives; their age is of no account. They shirk responsibility.

## The Trouble with the Sandwich

Mother came to tea. Big mistake by me, making sandwiches with cucumber in, even though I sliced it thin. She cried and was not willing to eat a sandwich with that filling. Father hated her to cry, but I did not mean to make him sigh. Or her to cry.

## Globally-Warmed Spring

Primroses in November, daffodils in December; the frogs return to my garden pond in croaking crowds, blue-throated males shouting for mates. Lumps of jelly spawn appear too soon and a late frost turns them white. The Silent Spring waits for no man, but frolicking frogs should wait for longer days.

# *Shiny*

## SALLY ANN NIXON

Don't know how I feel about Jamie. Sometimes I hate him. Most of the time, he is just around, quiet like. He's the one you see out the corner of your eye as you cross the road, pass a dark alley, glimpse in the corner as you toss in bed at night. He is usually a shy Jamie, never comes out fully, just shines for a second as a lure or a warning. And he has always been there. He has got me into trouble. I would follow Jamie wherever he led, and he led nowhere good, nowhere I wanted to go. He's led me into hospitals, courts, prison, one psychiatric unit after another. A malignant friend, despite his shyness. Now they've got the medication right. I think it helps, but Jamie never really goes away. Keeps catching me unawares.

Can't recall a time he wasn't with me. Once I found it comforting. Dad would shout at Mum, Mum would scream at Dad and they both threw things. Cups, plates, punches. I hid upstairs in bed, right under the covers, Jamie keeping me company. I asked him to keep me safe when I heard Mum sobbing and Dad lurching upstairs. I asked Jamie to be brave and bar the door so that Dad would forget me and crash by. Sometimes he did, sometimes he didn't, but however bad it got, Jamie stayed with me. He was my friend.

I moved out in my teens. Right away. The Social got me a room in a hostel and Jamie moved with me. It was a big room with a lock on the door. At home, I slept with door and window open so I could get out quick if I had to. Here I could lock Them out, whoever They were. And Jamie stood guard. I lay in bed listening to Nirvana and Coldplay, Jamie glinting above the door. I thought he would drive off intruders.

I talked to Jamie. He never answered, but I still knew he was there. I did wonder about Jamie now I had the time and safety to do it. Was he a sort of guardian angel, like Father Dermott told us about at school?

Or maybe he was my grandpa who died when I was five. I'd loved him and wept when he died.

Jamie followed me to college every day, a small shine at my elbow in the college kitchens as I learnt to cook and cater. I could see this little, silvery light. My friend. And life was good.

Until the day when Jamie betrayed me and troubles began. I stammer and They tease me when I stammer. Sometimes, I am clumsy. All fingers and thumbs, Mum said when she came to the open day. No Dad. Jamie had helped and he was long gone. Mum seemed proud of me, though, and Jamie shone a little brighter.

Then it happened.

We were in the college kitchens, all stainless steel and colour-coded boards. That kitchen gleamed and Jamie's shine was dimmed. I felt he didn't like it in there. He skulked in corners, tried to find dark places where there was no competition.

"Come on, Jamie," I muttered. "Jealousy won't get us anywhere."

Then it happened.

"Who you talkin' to? Mad, that's what you are, innit?"

Jamie flared – I felt it was almost gleeful – and They pushed and I slammed against the shiny, shiny stainless steel worktop. At the edge of my vision, Jamie was dancing round the knife block, flashing, spinning.

"Y-y-yer loopy, bro. Talkin' to no one there."

They pushed me again and the worktop cut into my back. In a bright blur, Jamie beckoned me on. I grabbed a knife, the one Jamie pushed to me, and one of Them lay on the floor. There was a lot of blood, on the shiny, shiny worktop, on the floor, on me. People were screaming, Mum was crying and Jamie dimmed to nothing behind me. I was pulled away, hauled away. Sirens, a van, shouting and I worried. Where was Jamie, my friend? Please don't desert me.

What happened then? I can hardly recall. There was a police cell, tea, a doctor, more tea. I kept asking for Jamie but They took me to the hospital instead. Time all mixed up together. There were pills, there were injections and bright lights but none of them were Jamie. There were people, kindly people, talking, talking.

Still, I had my own room, a white, clean room with a wired window so I could see out. There was a television. I'd never had my own before. And one day there was Jamie, in the corner as usual, watching me with no eyes. Funny, that. Strange that I never noticed that. I greeted him.

"Hey, old buddy. How you been?"

Jamie flared briefly, then settled down. But I knew things were changing.

I can never decide if that room was in a hospital or a prison. I was locked in, walked to therapy groups, given medication, interviewed, threatened, cajoled. I'm still on the pills and always will be. I don't go near knives. If I do, Jamie starts to dance and whirl and gets into my brain and I do bad things. Or imagine I do. I can't tell.

I have a job now, with other people from my hostel. It's at a recycling place. Jamie comes along but if I take my pills and go for my jab, he isn't a nuisance. We sort out the tins and bottles. The tins are bright and shiny. They gleam under the lights. But we don't like the manager. He nags at us and thinks I'm slow and finishes my word for me when I stammer. Jamie watches us from on top of a pile of rubbish. Watches with no eyes. He flares. He beckons me. The stainless steel tins gleam and glitter and Jamie is dancing.

"Jamie?"

# *Wounds*

BARBARA EVANS

The wounds of life will tear your face
And weigh upon your youthful grace.
The work of strife will bend your bones,
As if you're hung about with stones.
The turmoil that you feel within
Will pinch your guts and make them thin.

Then knots will grip your organs tight,
The pain will give you restless nights.
But the pain that's greater than the rest
Is the one that blundered from your breast.
When things you said caused others pain
Which you could not take back again.

It doesn't matter what you do,
Living isn't good for you.

# A Tale of Christmas

### LYNDA HOTCHKISS

Joey opened his eyes and looked around. For a moment he did not know where he was, then it all came back to him. The Romans. A head count. Travelling back to Bethlehem just as his wife was due to drop their first child. And that was another bone of contention! He hadn't touched his new wife since the day they were married, yet here she was with a swollen belly. By the time he found out she was expecting, it was too late to do anything about it. Besides, if he was totally honest, he quite liked having a woman around again. It had been several years since his previous wife had died, and it was hard work bringing up their boys. Not much work for carpenters these days!

He swung his legs off the straw mound on which he had slept for the past few hours. The journey had been hard with the constant moaning and groaning from his significant other half. As if it was his fault that he had to go back to where he was born! He had spent years trying to get away, finally finding a good job in Nazareth, and now he was back again, complete with spouse. Oh yes, and a donkey that she had insisted he buy for her. He had budgeted carefully for the journey but had to spend half of it on a flea-bitten quadruped because she found it difficult to walk at the same pace as him. He had haggled hard, but the farmer had got the better of him. Showed him one donkey but sold him an ass. That's Jewish businessmen for you! Drive a hard bargain that always comes out in their favour. Still, it had managed to get them here, and his wife had stopped moaning so much. She still groaned and grunted, though.

"Oy vay!" said Joey as something suddenly tapped him on the shoulder. He turned round to come face to face with a cow, a large beige cow with bad breath. Joey winced and wiped his brow with the back of his sleeve.

"Now I remember!" he said out loud. "Damn the census! Couldn't get a room for love nor money. Or rather for money or more money!"

He shrugged his shoulders, scratched his nether regions and finally got to his feet. Enjoying a good stretch, he leaned against the door frame and stared out at the yard where people were busily going to and fro.

"Looks like we're in for another hot day," he called over his shoulder.

Nobody said anything – except for a couple of horses, who whinnied quietly, hoping he would be bringing them a bag of oats.

"Is there anything you want?" he called again. "Breakfast? Foot rub? Oranges in wine?"

Only the soft bleating of sheep greeted his request.

He turned around and looked at where his wife lay sleeping. Or rather where she had been sleeping last night! All that remained of her presence was a slight dint in the straw.

"Where's she wandered off to now?" he mumbled with some disgruntlement.

Before he could make the slightest effort to find her, there came a strange strangled mewling sound from the deepest recess of the building. He followed the sound, and found his missing spouse cradling a new-born child in her arms.

The baby was wrapped in her scarf, and was still smeared with blood from the birth, but he could see it was a handsome child.

"You OK?" he said casually.

She nodded.

"And... and... it?"

She lifted her head and smiled at him before nodding again. That damned smile! It melted his heart every time he saw it, and now she had a babe in her arms it was even more haunting than before. Men would worship a woman with a smile like hers!

"A boy," she said sweetly, her attention returning to the child. "You have a son, husband."

He opened his mouth to refute that fact, but thought better of it. Instead, he knelt down before mother and child and placed one work-roughened finger under the small pink fist that had escaped from the swaddling. The infant curled its tiny fingers around it and, in that instant, Joey loved it as if it was his own flesh and blood. Admittedly, he was thinking how soon the boy would be able to help in the workshop once they returned home, but for now the three of them were alone in an animal shed, with only a few beasts for company. The next few hours would be theirs before the world intruded in the form of well-meaning visitors, and the rest of their lives would become history.

# Four Haiku

PETER CORRIN

Three lines? Pithy words?
Seventeen syllables long?
Must be a haiku!

My lips still feel yours
Even as you walk away
I know you love me

Peaceful sleeping cat
Chasing mice and stalking birds
In her twitching dreams

Golden rose of dawn
Ushers in a blue-sky day
In winter? Freezing!

# The TRUE Story of George and the Dragon

## BRIAN HUMPHREYS

'Do you have to do that in the house?' asked George's wife. 'I've told you before. If you must polish your helmet, do it outside.'

'Yes, milady,' he said sarcastically, gathering up several pieces of armour. George loved his fair maiden, warts and all.

She followed him into the courtyard. 'Does this activity mean that you're off gallivanting, *again?*'

'I'd hardly call slaying a dragon "gallivanting".'

'I'm sick of eating dragon. Can't you slay a cow for a change?'

'But I'm George the dragon-slayer, not George the cow-slayer.'

'Well, don't bring the dragon's carcase home, because I won't cook it, and another thing: on your way home, can you call in at the chemist's? I need some more wart cream.'

With a flea in his ear and a shopping list in his pocket, George rode into the village, his well-polished armour glinting in the morning sun. As he neared the community centre, he saw a large dragon with eyes like red coals and a mouth that breathed fire. His trusty steed also saw the large dragon, and emptied its bowels. George encouraged his trusty steed a little nearer, raised his lance, and prepared to charge. 'For England and Saint George,' he shouted.

A man stepped out, blocking his way. 'Stop right there,' the man ordered. 'Is that your horse?'

George looked down between his legs. 'I've never seen it before in my life, good sir.'

The man ignored George's sarcasm. 'Have you just ridden along Pastures Avenue?'

George replied with the patience of a saint. 'Yes, but I kept well within the speed limit.'

'We operate a green policy in this village because we care about our environment, so unless you go back and poop-scoop the mess that your horse deposited outside number 36, I'll have you thrown into the stocks – and what, may I ask, is your business in this village?'

'I'm a dragon-slayer, about to kill yonder dragon.'

The dragon snarled, setting fire to the man's clipboard.

'Do you have a permit?' asked the man, dropping his flaming clipboard.

'A permit? I don't need a permit. I'm Saint George, the patron saint of England.'

'If we eventually release Squire Mead's 106 agreement money and build a suitable arena, then, and only then, might we permit jousting and fights to the death. Until that time, there'll be no killing without council approval.'

'Council approval!' exclaimed Saint George. 'Who are you to tell me that I need approval?'

'I'm chairman of the parish council, and if you want to register a complaint or obtain a permit, put it in writing to the parish clerk.'

And so, the 'legendary' fight between Saint George and the dragon *did not* take place in the village of St Georges. However, the following week, in the village of Yatton where anything goes, the fight *did* take place and the dragon was duly slain.

# David

## JENNY MURPHY

When you left me today, Mum, I realised how I long to tell you how much I appreciate all the care you have given me over the years, and how much I really love you, but even though you understand me more than anyone else does, the sign language would be too complicated for you to grasp. Telling you that I love you is fine, but the depth of that love would be impossible for me to describe.

You must think that I am unhappy; it isn't true. I have accepted now that my life must be lived through others. I do enjoy following the progress of John at work as an accountant and Jean away at university. Their triumphs have become my own, but I do miss being able to discuss them; to chat proudly about my big brother and sister, as others do.

Often, I hear staff talking and showing photographs of their children as they grow older. Of course, I show my album of writing and photos to whoever can be bothered to look, but my responses to questions remain monosyllabic. No matter what I am thinking, others decide for me. Take last Wednesday, for example. The enormous care-staff girl Margaret said to me, 'Come on, David, let's have a bath!' The very thought of the two of us together in the water made me bubble inside with laughter and I thrashed my arms about to try to make her see the joke. It didn't work. She looked at me in such a concerned fashion. I'm sure she thought I was having a fit.

I'm glad everybody seems to have dropped the subject of my behavioural problems. I always did feel it was strange to be given a label more appropriate for a toddler. I suppose, when I was a few years younger, I hadn't accepted what my life would be like. I was sure that, one day, I would wake up and find that the whole world understood.

I feel guilty now to think how I resented John and Jean growing up and moving on. I'm not the same, and neither will I ever be.

Sometimes, when they are at home, they talk of going out for meals with friends. I listen and think how wonderful it would be not to have to rely on a nurse giving me small amounts of pocket money from some hidden cupboard. If only – and I promise that this is the only one – if only I could go on a spending spree and choose outrageous clothing, and not that easily put on and removed. I would go to a top restaurant and order whatever I liked, without considering the balance needed to assist my bowels. I've lost track of the meals that I didn't want and didn't order being passed off as my choice, and even assisted into my mouth.

For the moment, life seems to be on the up. More people are trying to understand and are learning to communicate with me. It gives me a buzz and makes me feel so important when someone makes the effort.

Finally, Mum, I hope I haven't upset you, but when I lie in bed at night, I speak inside my head to my real father. If what the priest told me is true, then one day, I will be able to communicate with him and you with ease. So, for now, I store up my jokes and day-to-day incidents to share with him. I feel him smiling at my quick wit and laughing at the antics of the staff.

So always remember, Mum, that I love you for your care, and even though I will never be able to tell you, except with my eyes, I always will.

# *Last Man Standing*

## GUY JENKINSON

*FLAK! I'M HIT! Black smoke erupts from the shattered cowling; the engine falters and dies.*

*ON FIRE! Bright orange flame blasts the oil-spattered windshield as the nose drops into a steep dive. Fear is like a blow to the stomach – panic numbs the mind!*

*GOING DOWN! Instinct coincides with training: unplug the helmet RT lead, snatch the harness quick-release; an incandescent torrent of fire streams past the cockpit: like a blast-furnace, driven by a 400mph slipstream.*

*BAIL OUT! Desperately wrench the canopy release; the universe fills with sound: a scream, then a huge roar that obliterates all thought in a tidal wave of noise...*

*BLACKNESS!*

Sir Lawrence awoke with a start, disorientated and, for a few seconds, confused.

Two hundred metres away, a Eurofighter lifted off from the main runway, then pointed its nose at the heavens as its pilot engaged full afterburner for a nearly vertical climb: the ground shook, as eighteen tonnes of thrust hurled the aircraft skywards.

Slowly, his awareness returned: he was sitting on a wooden bench outside the visitor centre of RAF Coningsby; it was late in the afternoon of Battle of Britain Day, 2005, and Sir Lawrence – the Commandant's VIP guest – was resting to catch his breath.

He had been invited to Coningsby to observe the new Eurofighter, now officially called the Typhoon, being introduced into full squadron service.

Wryly, Sir Lawrence wondered if someone in the RAF's personnel department had discovered that his war service included Typhoons... the 1940s Napier piston-engined variety.

Earlier, he had slipped away from the official tour to visit the base's cemetery, a small, pristine enclosure of immaculate headstones and manicured grass, nestling against the airfield's boundary fence.

The walk had tired him. "We who are left grow old!" he murmured to himself.

*We who are left grow old! Old indeed, but at least I'm still here. "Every dawn you see is a victory"; who said that? So many brave young warriors never enjoyed the peace for which we all fought – unless one counts eternal peace, of course... and they live on in memory for as long as I remember them.*

"Ah, Sir Lawrence – I've finally caught up with you!" A cultured voice with a cut-glass Oxbridge accent intruded into the old man's reverie. "My name's Cornwall, sir – Flight Lieutenant Sebastian Cornwall."

Startled, he looked up to see a tall, blond young man standing over him, sporting a luxuriant moustache that made it hard to estimate his real age. Sir Lawrence made eye contact and, for a few seconds, returned the other man's unblinking gaze whilst noting the pale – almost icy – blue of his irises: hunter's eyes! Assessing the newcomer's lean build and alert stance, he guessed the Flight Lieutenant was in his late twenties... thirty, perhaps.

Despite the warm afternoon, Cornwall was wearing an old-style leather flying jacket; Sir Lawrence couldn't see any indication of rank but, under the leather coat, on the lapel of the Flight Lieutenant's uniform he glimpsed several medal ribbons, including – to his surprise – the distinctive blue and white diagonals of the coveted Distinguished Flying Cross.

"Cornwall?" Sir Lawrence cocked his head. "That name sounds familiar – I was once on a short course with a Flying Officer

Cornwall... back in '42, as I recall. Any relation? Your grandfather, perhaps?" he added, jokingly.

Cornwall simply extended his hand, gushing: "It's such an honour to meet you, Sir Lawrence... it's not often that a chap gets the opportunity to chin-wag with such a legendary pilot."

Taking Cornwall's proffered hand, Sir Lawrence laughed self-deprecatingly. "Ancient aeroplane driver, certainly; I don't know about being legendary!"

"Nevertheless, sir, if you don't mind, I'd like to talk to you about your career."

Resigning himself to being interviewed, Sir Lawrence stood up, leant on his walking sticks and reflected painfully that if wisdom comes with age then so does arthritis. "OK, Flight Lieutenant Cornwall, you can accompany me as I walk off the stiffness of encroaching years and we'll talk a bit – although I must say, I can't see that I'm all that interesting... I'm just a relic of a forgotten era – perhaps the last of my kind!"

"One thing, sir; would you mind calling me Seb? Everyone else does."

"Very well, Seb – so, what do you want to know?"

Cornwall pulled out a battered pocketbook and rifled through it, saying, "Well, sir, I already know that you served in the RAF during the war, flying Typhoons..."

Sir Lawrence smiled and nodded, his suspicions about the motive for his invitation now confirmed.

"...then, after the war, you stayed on, flying Meteors and Vampires. You had a distinguished career as a test pilot, responsible for advances in high-performance fighter development. You flew fast jets into your mid-fifties and you were still flying when you retired, aged sixty-three."

*Ye gods! Was it really that long – gaining my wings in February*

*1943 to my retirement in July 1987 – that's, what... nearly four and a half **decades** of risking my neck in aeroplanes... yet it seems to have passed in an instant. Somewhere in there, I got a degree, married and raised three children.*

Slowly, the pair walked towards the main runway until, self-consciously, Cornwall realised that Sir Lawrence had noticed his rather pronounced limp. Looking up, he felt the older man's voiceless question in his expression.

Cornwall shrugged. "Stopped a bit of shrapnel in Iraq," he said. "Nothing too serious, though."

"What happened, Seb? Flak?" asked Sir Lawrence. "Jaguar or Tornado?"

"Neither," replied Cornwall. "We'd been seconded to Habbaniya airbase; I was hit during an op when we bounced an Iraqi rebel column fleeing towards Fallujah. We were running short of aircrew and I'd been co-opted as a door gunner."

Sir Lawrence nodded sympathetically. "Door gunner, eh – on a Chinook?" he asked.

"No, a Valentia."

Sir Lawrence was trying to place this unfamiliar aircraft type when Seb peered at his watch, then interjected: "I am very sorry to rush you, sir, but we do need to keep to the schedule. The rest of your tour awaits... and it's meant to be a surprise!"

"The rest of...?" Sir Lawrence said, surprised. "Where to now, Seb? I thought we'd covered almost the entire base during this morning's guided tour... in minute detail!"

"Yes, sir, that we did; all I can say is that this bit involves a Dakota."

"A Douglas DC-3 Dakota, indeed!" Sir Lawrence chuckled. "OK, Seb, where did you get that museum piece – from the Battle of Britain Memorial Flight?"

"Not exactly. This one was borrowed by special arrangement so you could enjoy some exclusive transport to a reunion; we've rounded up a few bods from your RAF days." Smiling broadly, he continued, "Anyway, this will be a much less formal do than the Commandant's bash – and with fewer brass-hats present!"

They reached the now silent and empty runway; Cornwall looked up and down its length, then said, "Our kite's not here yet, sir, so we've got a few minutes to wait; that's OK, as I really want to find out about the Four Musketeers flight... that is, if you don't mind talking about it."

*"Four Musketeers" – my old flight: "Snowy", "Skid", "Sharky" and me, "Long" Standing; what a crew! I haven't thought about them in years, not since the war... no, not since '94, when I read that Marlin had finally shuffled off this mortal coil, fifty years after the other two.*

Leaning on his sticks, Sir Lawrence gazed into the distance, deliberately avoiding looking at Cornwall. "No, Seb, I don't mind at all," he said, as a tear glistened on his cheek; surreptitiously, he wiped it away. Suddenly weary, he carefully lowered his spare frame onto the mown grass, alongside the tarmac; after a few seconds, Cornwall sat down cross-legged beside him and opened his notebook.

"Now, sir, I'd like to hear all about the legendary Musketeers flight – I gather that was just an unofficial nickname?" asked Cornwall.

"Yes, it certainly was," replied Sir Lawrence. "Officially, it was simply 'A' flight, but that was how we saw ourselves – as warriors... as knights of the air, fighting in a just crusade against a monstrous evil." He smiled enigmatically, his gaze focusing on some distant point as he savoured his memories before continuing, "It was such fun, as well!"

For the next twenty minutes or so, Sir Lawrence described his companions to a fascinated Cornwall: he recalled how his youthful fellow warriors had flown the mighty Typhoon fighter-bombers that inflicted grievous destruction on the enemy.

He related the story of Wilfred Baker-Jones, who was also known as

Snowy. After his fiancée died in a sneak attack on a seaside town by a Focke-Wulf 190 intruder, Jones had lived only to kill... and to die, as he drove his crippled aircraft into the side of a blazing tanker during a shipping strike off Cherbourg.

*Yes – you crazy bastard! They awarded you a posthumous DFC for that. I wept for you.*

Sir Lawrence spoke of Stephen "Skid" Hallingbury, killed in 1944 whilst testing a replacement Typhoon that suddenly dived into the ground at over 450mph.

*Yes, I remember your remains were poured into a waterproof sack and returned to your family in a sealed coffin – with a note saying, "do NOT open".*

Finally, Sir Lawrence told Cornwall about the magnificently-named Josiah Wedgewood Marlin – nicknamed Sharky – who survived the war to die peacefully in his native Canada, half a century later.

*Dear old Sharky – and to think you'd wanted to become a priest!*

The air started to vibrate with the low-pitched rumble of aero engines.

*Wow! That takes me back! Wright Cyclones, nine-cylinder, air-cooled radials!*

Sir Lawrence looked up to see a twin-engined transport aircraft slowly taxiing towards them; it braked to a stop with engines idling.

"Ah, they're here, sir," announced Cornwall. With that, he helped Sir Lawrence to his feet and, taking his arm, guided him towards the waiting Dakota. A door opened in its rear fuselage as unseen hands deployed a short aluminium stepladder.

"All aboard, please – this way, sir!" called Cornwall, standing aside to allow Sir Lawrence to ascend first.

"I never imagined these old bones would get to ride again in an old kite like this!" said Sir Lawrence, smiling as he climbed the steps. Several shadowy figures reached out to assist his entry.

Outside the visitor centre, paramedics Marlowe and Bailey became aware of a distant rumble approaching from the south. The sound became louder, rising to an uneven, throbbing growl, then to a spine-tingling snarl: unmistakably Rolls-Royce Merlin engines – several of them!

They shielded their eyes to watch, as a flight of four Spitfires flew towards them in a rigid, asymmetric V-formation. Suddenly, one of the aircraft peeled off and headed west, towards the setting sun, whilst the others continued northwards.

"Interesting," said Marlowe. "That's one manoeuvre I've not seen before."

"Course you have, you ignorant sod," replied Bailey. "Have you never seen a Missing Man formation? It's flown to honour a dead pilot!" He paused. "Mind you, I thought the Memorial Flight ran a mixed bag of Spits from Mark II to Mark XIX – I could swear that those four were all Mark IXs... and they were all in D-Day markings, as well."

As he spoke, a sudden surge of noise from different engines added to the din.

He looked again to the south, where a Dakota was lifting off the main runway, heading west towards the sunset. With engines at full power, struggling to gain height, it banked into a steep climbing turn to port until it could head north, after the Spitfires.

It passed overhead, low enough for the paramedics to see the two pilots and, peering out of the fuselage windows, five or six passengers.

As they watched, the Dakota climbed rapidly to join the three remaining fighters, which immediately took up station around it before the whole formation slowly wheeled to port and followed the first Spitfire into the setting sun.

The two men watched the retreating aircraft for a minute or so, then returned their attention to the body on the wooden bench.

"Well," said Marlowe, "I'm afraid there's nothing more we can do for him. Who was this fellow, anyway? He looks a bit distinguished... if you see what I mean."

Bailey rummaged in the dead man's jacket pocket and pulled out a dog-eared leather wallet; from it, he extracted a laminated ID card to which was clipped an official invitation.

"This says he's Sir Lawrence Standing... OBE, DFC, AFC, DFM – blimey, what a load of gongs! Crikey, he was a retired Air Commodore; well, he certainly went to his Maker from the right place, on the right day."

"Pity he's missing this fly-past, though," commented Marlowe.

Towards the west, the little formation vanished from sight as the sound of its engines diminished into eternal silence.

*Per ardua ad astra.*

# Shelley and Shane Find Their Way Home

## FAITH MOULIN

It was the anniversary of their first date and they were supposed to be moving in together. New town, new jobs, new life. Trouble was their new jobs started in two weeks' time and they hadn't found anywhere suitable to live. Shelley was tearful and tired.

"Perhaps this is the one," Shane said as they traipsed up another path to another dismal flat.

Shane shook hands with the landlord of the so-called 'luxury apartment'. He knew by now that 'luxury' meant 're-painted in white with a clean carpet'. It was still only one room, a studio flat with a bath like a cattle trough in it. A large plasma-screen TV dominated one wall.

"At least you could watch TV while you had a bath," whispered Shane. Shelley frowned. The landlord was explaining that the toilet was down the corridor, shared with another flat. She frowned again.

"You don't live in the toilet, do ya?" said the landlord, scratching at the tattoo on his forearm. It was a grinning shark.

Shane looked at Shelley. "We'll need to think about it," he said.

"Nuffin' to fink about, sunshine. Take it or leave it. I've got two more viewings later."

They left it.

Shane had borrowed his father's satnav for the property search. "Let's go to the Green Dragon in Hertford and get something to eat," he said. He had been there once before. Shelley found it on the screen. Brilliant. Only two dead ends and a deep ford and they were there.

Feeling less desperate over steak and ale pie, the young couple decided to go home and talk to Shane's parents about borrowing some money for a deposit. "We can't rent. We'll need to buy," said Shane. "They'll understand, they'll lend it if they've got it."

Shelley bit her lip. "But it doesn't solve the immediate problem of where to live when we start our jobs."

They were both subdued as they drove away from the town. Shane was angry about the property market, angry he couldn't get his foot on the so-called ladder. It wasn't even that he wanted to go up in the world; he just wanted to live there now, without making some leech of a landlord rich and himself poor.

Shelley was just sad. She wanted to make a home – to choose her own feather cushions and pizza toppings. She pressed *Home* on the satnav and off they went to find the M1.

Sometimes ring roads and one-way streets take off in what appears to be the wrong direction, so they weren't unduly worried to start with. Then: "Turn round," Shelley said. "This isn't right. We're going north."

Shane turned abruptly into a tree-lined road and immediately on their left was a beautiful Edwardian house in a fine state of repair where a man was just erecting a *To Let* sign. Shane stopped the car and they both wordlessly descended on the man. Neither had much hope of avoiding another knock-back.

It was just on the market, available in two weeks, the most clean and comfortable place they had seen. "Two months' rent and it's yours," said the polite and cheerful owner.

Shane's phone beeped. Shelley beamed at her new landlord. "It's a lovely place," she said. "It feels just like home."

"Sorry, excuse me," Shane said, and he read the text from his dad: *"Satnav not programmed for home."*

*Not your home, anyway,* Shane thought.

*"Thanks, Dad,"* he replied. *"Satnav knew best. All good here. Home by 9."*

# *Forget-me-not*

## VICTORIA HELEN TURNER

A million million years ago, when the earth was new and as fresh as the dewy grass in the pearl-grey dawn, when the blue of heaven was reflected in the eyes of birds and beasts, and men and women truly lived in the ways of the Creator – there were certain angels who turned away from God and all that was good. They had discovered the negative force and they became evil. The leader of these angels and his followers fell down from heaven, down, down, into a hell of their own making, from where they tormented human beings for evermore and tortured the souls of those who had fallen into evil ways.

Not all the fallen angels had reached hell; some had repented too late, but the Creator took pity on them and allowed them to alight on the earth to live as elementals because they were not good enough for heaven, or bad enough for hell. Wherever the fallen angels landed, blue flowers sprang from the earth, the blue of heaven. They were called forget-me-nots, a reminder that never again must they forget their Lord. To atone for their evil, they helped human beings to keep in the ways of God, and in time they were known as the fair folk – the fairies!

By only one way could a fairy regain entrance to heaven. If a human loved and married one, then the fairy would become human and gain an immortal soul, and in the course of time die, and return to heaven.

One day, in the land of Hyporborea, the young King Ranaldus, handsome, black of hair and eye, was riding past a small lake of delicate clear water. In a forest clearing, a maiden knelt by the lake washing her gown. Her hair, silver blonde, shone like the glaciers of the great north land, and her eyes were as blue as the forget-me-nots that blossomed by the lakeside. Ronaldus knew that she was a fallen angel, a fairy, but he loved her. The maiden's name was Sorrel, and she loved Ronaldus the moment she saw him. She put on her wet green gown, and the droplets fell into the lake like tears of happiness from heaven.

The king lifted Sorrel onto his horse, and took her to his home, a castle on a high mountain, where they married and she gained her immortal soul. In the years that followed, she told her children and her children's children to always remember that forget-me-nots are the living trace of the presence of fallen angels!

*This story was inspired by a Scottish legend of the forget-me-not.*

# Tapeworm

## SALLY ANN NIXON

Jimbo was tough. Loved Bear Grylls. Worshipped the SAS. Went on survival courses, picked up road kill and had breath like a sulphur pit. I had known him since school and he had not improved with time. Jimbo was fond of saying how he could survive anything, eat anything, no problem.

"Look at all those wusses on the telly. Making a fuss over a few termites. Pansies."

Jimbo was tough. He also thought himself irresistible, despite the foul breath, the BO – soap is for wimps – and the food-flecked stubble. Jimbo was a real man, looking for a real woman.

I hated him. Always had. Hell was his calloused thumb on my doorbell and his blotched red face peering through the window. I asked him to dinner, gave him the chance to show off. He played right into it.

"Just you and me, eh?" He leered happily, rasping fumes across the table.

I simpered and passed him a plate. Dried tapeworm: my dog was so obliging. Poor thing tossed with butter and white wine, laced with just a little aconite from the garden and sprinkled with a soupçon of deathcap from the woods behind the house. I smiled coyly. "Of course. A recipe of my own, all taken from Mother Nature. I know your tastes so well."

Jimbo accepted the dish. "All for me! No, not your sort of thing, you townees."

He tucked in greedily. I waited and with real relish watched as his face darkened, he choked and began to foam at the mouth.

"Nice one, Jimbo. Death by tapeworm."

# New Beginning

PETER CORRIN

Like a cowering butterfly emergent
From the safety of its chrysalis,
So, from behind walls and shields and armour,
So at last come I, but reticent.
Fears of unknown, history still strident,
Carapace too tight for further dwelling,
Keeping up the artifice too tiring,
Seeking still the path that has been meant.
Still the echoes of the long-held, bold face
Mingle with the new in rare confusion
As the metamorphosis takes place,
It gradually sees the old ways razed
And the naked psyche, in transition,
Steps slowly to the light, its hope unfazed.

# *Caring Christmas*

### SALLY ANN NIXON

I don't know why I'm here. I should be home with my mum, my brother and my nan. It's not bad here, though. They try. They try too hard. Anyway, what's all this Christmas peace and goodwill thing about?

I've been with them to loads of things. We did Christingle at the church. We did the panto – free tickets for kids in care. We did a candle carol service at the church. There was a kids' party at that church too. Never been in a church and it smells funny. Old-fashioned party it was, all cribs and party games and party food and lemonade. Lemonade. Who makes their own lemonade these days? The church lot do. We said a prayer thing at the start and had a Christmas quiz about this baby in a stable. Knew a bit about that, as I've seen it on the telly. Sang a song about a donkey too. Baby should have been in care, and donkey should have gone to a refuge place, if you ask me.

Anyway. Here I am. It's early but there are people moving about. Got a tree downstairs, with a load of presents under it. The radio's on. More Christmas carols. I put my head round the door and there's a big, red stocking, like Nan used to do, hanging on the knob.

*"Matt. Happy Christmas from Father Christmas."*

Like I believe in that.

Well, it's mine, though. Let's see.

Chocolate... a torch... a kit to make a wooden spider... funny socks... an orange... felt tips.

No PlayStation game. Hoped I'd get FIFA. Maybe it's under the tree.

Why am I here? At home, I'd be down watching TV. Mum and her new boyfriend wouldn't be up for hours and Nathan and me would be eating Coco Pops out the packet. Nan'd come over in a bit and put the Christmas dinner on. She'd have been to Iceland like on the telly and there'd be a chicken, 'cause we don't like turkey, and some roast tatties and peas and gravy. Nan's chocolate pudding after with ice cream. And lots of Pepsi. After, Mum'd get out the strawberry voddie and her and what's-'is-name would go back to bed and watch DVDs. Nan'd wash up and we'd help and we'd all cuddle up on the couch and watch the old films Nan likes till we fall asleep. No need to get dressed even. Not all day. It's home.

Why am I here? I know why. Nan, she got sick and had to go into a care home. Nathan and me, Mum's new boyfriend didn't like us, told Mum it was us or him. So we went. Don't know where Nathan is but they said we could meet up in New Year at the Resource Centre. Maybe Mum will come without whatsit. So I'm here with these people who get paid for looking after me, want me to be like them, want me to like what they like, and I don't. I try but I don't. I want Nathan and Nan and my mum.

I go downstairs. It's all bright and there's this calendar thing with a picture that you open every day and one last chocolate in it for me. I've new Christmas slippers. Funny ones that look like hairy puppies. Not had slippers before and they feel strange. There's mince pies and sausage rolls. I like sausage rolls for breakfast. Ouch. It's really hot. She gives me some juice. Everyone's smiling. Great big turkey on the side, all stuffed and tied up like something in a hospital. I poke it with my finger and it gives and I don't fancy it.

"That the bird?" I ask.

"Yup. That's our Christmas meal," he says. "It'll look better when it's cooked."

The telly is off. What are we supposed to do without telly? I look round. There's that pile of stuff under the tree. I wonder if I can find mine and open it. Hope it's a game.

"Matt. Matt. We've a surprise for you, Matt."

Don't like surprises. They usually mean trouble. They scare me. But she's smiling and holding out a ball of red wool.

"Follow the wool, Matt."

So I laugh – that's what they want, I think – and I follow the wool. There's a trail of it. Out of the kitchen, into the hall, round into the loo, into the big room and round the tree. It goes on and on. The dopey dog follows it, too. Is there a bone at the end? Is that the surprise? Wool goes through the garden door and down the path. It's wet. Slippers off, trainers on. Out past the bins and down to the shed.

Oh, WOW. It's a bike! A new one from the shop. A BMX, like Nathan had. It's mine. There's a helmet and a card thing saying, *"Happy Christmas to dear Matt."* It's mine. My BMX. A red BMX.

Can't bear this. I hide in the corner of the shed and pull up my hood and cry. I want my Nan and Nathan and my mum to see it and the sausage rolls and the dopey dog that licks my face and tells me it's all OK. It'll all be OK.

"Come on, Matt."

I wheel my red bike up to the kitchen and she gives me a tissue and a cuddle and more juice and some cereal.

The telly is on. It's a cartoon with snowmen dancing. Then I can open my presents under the tree and there is my game, and some Lego and a jumper with a reindeer and a hat. Whoo.

Banging on the door. I can smell the turkey cooking. There's people coming in for a drink and grown-up children and a baby. The dopey dog gets excited and shut in the kitchen. More Christmas music and a lot of cheering and laughing. The dog is let out and even he has a bone. I'm lost. I go and sit by my bike in the kitchen, nibble a sausage roll, cold this time, and hug the dog who seems to know how lonely I'm feeling.

"Merry Christmas! Happy Christmas! Merry Christmas."

All lights and paper hats and crackers and this fizzy wine. It's loud and noisy and great, really it is. But I want the flat and Coco Pops, Nan and Nathan and Mum, and they will never be there again.

# A Woman's Work

## FAITH MOULIN

"I can't abide pink slippers. I'm not a tart!" Irene's mother said.

It was hard enough to buy slippers for gnarled, old, arthritic feet without having to worry about colour discrimination. Now Irene would have to take them back. Impossible shopping feats were down to her now. She spent hours in town at the emporiums for the elderly looking for things like long-legged flannelette knickers and slippers that weren't pink. There was no time to shop for her own clothes.

Irene was trying to hold her marriage together, hold down her job and leave hold of her adult children, who were driving her mad with their demands. The last thing she needed was another drama at her mother's. As she put down the phone she purposefully reconstructed a memory of her mother as a kind, caring, empathetic and helpful person. It wasn't entirely as she remembered things, but Irene liked to do the right thing and she felt she should be trying to return decades of love from the older-than-old woman into whom her mother had transformed, almost overnight. Irene had hoped her mother would come to terms with the pink slippers, given a few hours and her failing eyesight.

Irene had once visited an ancient tree. It was believed to be over two thousand years old. "Nearly as old as you, Mum," she had joked that day. Her mother was only in her eighties then and still on her own two feet. Now those feet had encrustations and knobbly eruptions just like the old tree. They had contorted with age, tiny foot bones supporting shiny marble-like growths under the taut, thin skin. Other areas were callused with thick flaky skin like plaques of veteran bark.

The feet were of no use now, much like the rest of the skeletal remains that were her mother. Irene was sorry for her but sometimes she also felt a little twinge of resentment. She felt one now as she shouted to Don, "I'm just popping to Mum's on my way to work. Bye!"

Irene's mother lived in a small convenient group of old people's bungalows just round the corner. Irene picked up the milk from the step on her way into the bungalow and shouted, "Hello!" loudly. That was the routine. She did that so as not to startle the old woman who didn't always hear the door open. She looked at the carers' notes on the kitchen worktop left for her daily perusal. Yesterday's read: *All good. Please buy more toilet rolls.*

"Thank God you've come!" her mother said.

Irene winced. "The carer will be along soon, Mum."

"I don't like her handling me like a piece of meat. Couldn't you stay and help me get dressed? Just this once." She whined it out like a spoilt child asking for more sweets. "Please, Irene."

"No, the carer will dress you, Mum. What was the other thing? You rang me because you said the gardener had found something."

"God, yes," said her mother, remembering the importance of the issue. "I wanted to ring you last night but I quite forgot by the time the carer had finished all her flapping and fussing."

"Tell me, then. I've got to get to work," Irene said, reaching into her store of patience for just a few more grains of a scarce commodity.

"It was the boy who looks after the garden for me. He found a snake. The back door was open and when he emptied the compost bin there was a snake in it and it moved so fast he didn't know where it went. He said it might have come in the house – into the kitchen, he said."

Irene sighed. "I don't think a snake would like to come into the house, Mum," she said, "but I'll have a good look-round just to make sure."

Where would a snake go? Would it go to a dark place to hide, or would it be attracted to warmth and light and try to find its way back outside? She lay on her front and looked under the fridge. It was filthy under there. Guilt welled up in Irene's throat like vomit and she had to swallow it. She hadn't cleaned under there for months – perhaps it was even years. She got a torch and looked under the washing machine too, thinking it was all very well having a cleaner but they didn't do the difficult areas. She had to do all those, dragging out the sofa, cleaning the windows. She didn't have time for those jobs at home but she had to do them round here.

"No sign of it in the kitchen," she shouted.

Her mother shouted back, "What are you looking for, dear?"

Irene went into the dining room where a sliding patio door led outside. She looked under the sideboard and then gave a glance around the other rooms. It was nearly eight o'clock. She needed to get going.

Her mother was calling her. "What's going on, Irene?"

"Nothing," she said. "There's no snake in the house. Nothing to worry about."

Her mobile phone was ringing in her handbag. It was Don.

"Can you get some toilet rolls on the way home?" he said.

"Can't you? I'm really busy tonight. I've got to meet the grandchildren from school and come back round here to check up on Mum's medication."

"Take the kids to the shops with you."

"I'd rather not. They'll want sweets."

She could hear the annoyance in her husband's silence.

"All right," she said, terminating the call.

"Who're you talking to?" called her mother from her bed. "What's going on?"

"Nothing, Mum," she said, making her way to the bedroom. "I'll call in later with Jack and Jodie. That'll be nice, won't it?" She kissed her mother on the cheek and closed her ears to any more delaying tactics.

Eight hours later she let the boisterous children into her mother's bungalow. She had fuelled them with cheap lollipops and jelly frogs.

"Hello, Great Grandma!" shouted Jack while he took his shoes off. He had a favourite question for her which he always enjoyed because she never gave him the same answer twice. "How old are you today?"

Irene interpreted her mother's silence as confusion. Poor old thing had probably been asleep and didn't know how old she was.

Jack continued, "I'm seven!" Then he called Irene in a different voice. It sounded panicky. Irene and Jodie followed him into the lounge where they found a large African woman face-down on the floor. It was Precious, the carer from Zimbabwe who weighed in at over twenty stone. Irene's mother was nowhere to be seen.

"Find Great Grandma!" Irene yelled. She was trying to visualise size and volume so she could work out whether her frail mother would fit under Precious without any part of her showing. The thought of it passed through her like a skewer.

Irene was relieved when the children found her mother asleep in her bed. They soon put an end to that. Her mother woke up with a start and began complaining loudly about the carers who had not come to get her up and left her stuck in bed all day long. Irene was meanwhile trying to roll Precious over, but this lady was not for turning. Not by her, anyway. The soft plush black skin was warm, however, so she wasn't dead. Irene reached for her phone as her mother called, "Irene! Don't leave me in here with these children! What's going on?"

"Nothing, Mum," said Irene. "Nothing to worry about," and she called an ambulance.

Irene's mobile phone was ringing. It was her daughter Hannah.

"Are the kids OK?" she asked. "Do you think you could pick up some toilet rolls for me when you bring them back? We're almost out and I shan't have time to get to the shops."

"OK," said Irene. "Must dash."

She noticed the smell as soon as she entered her mother's room. "It stinks in here," she said.

"It's Great Grandma," said Jodie.

"The carer didn't come. I couldn't get up to go to the toilet," said her mother. "You know I can't get up out of bed without help."

Irene rang Don. "You'll have to come and get the kids," she said.

"I can't."

"Mum's wet the bed."

Jack was now standing by the dressing table. He was trying to pull the head off the little wooden ballerina on the jewellery box. Jodie was stroking her great grandma's hair. The old woman hated people touching her hair and was swatting at the child with a claw-like hand and snapping, "Stop it! Stop it!"

"The carer should have seen to all that," Don said.

"The carer's out cold on the floor," Irene said. "I've called an ambulance."

Don still prevaricated. "I'm in the middle of something."

Irene wasn't falling for that one. She could hear the television in the background. "Don, please!"

He hung up, beaten for once by the drama of the circumstances.

"Nanna!" called Jodie from the bathroom. "There's no toilet paper."

When the paramedics had taken Precious off to hospital and Don had taken his grandchildren home to watch a DVD, Irene got her mother up and washed her and changed her clothes. The old woman was subdued. She had been frightened by the paramedics, with their loud voices and big bags. She thought they had come to take her away.

"I hate being old," she told Irene, not for the first time.

"I know you do," said Irene. "Let's get you in the dining room while I change the bed. It's warm in there."

She was still sorting out her mother's bed when she heard her calling, "What's going on?"

"Nothing, Mum," she replied.

"Yes there is. Something's gone wrong with the door."

Irene abandoned the half-made bed and went to the dining room. There was nothing wrong with the door.

"No, it's fine, Mum," she said, but her mother was pointing at the patio door.

"What's going on down there?" she asked.

Irene looked at the bottom of the door. She bent down to move a long thin piece of black rubber draught excluder which was lying in a wavy line along the frame. She couldn't think how the grandchildren had had time to wreck that, but she would have to try to push it back on.

"It's just the rubber strip on the bottom of the door, Mum," she said. "Nothing to worry about."

As she crouched down she saw it move. "Aaah!" she gasped.

Her mother asked, "What is it? What's going on?" just as Irene began to believe her eyes.

It wasn't a strip of rubber at all. It was a small snake! It had a beautiful yellow mark like a collar round its neck and Irene remembered that meant it was a harmless grass snake. With shaky hands she got a tissue box and tried to push the snake into it as it writhed and wriggled. Harmless or not, she wasn't sure she wanted to grab it directly.

"It's nothing, Mum. Don't worry," she said.

The snake was happy to slide into the box, but equally happy, in one long fluid movement, to slither out again. Irene felt its smooth skin against her fingers, its muscles rippling, pushing for freedom, eager for the outside world. Her mobile phone was ringing. She left the box and snake while she answered it. A nurse was calling to let her know that Precious would be staying in hospital overnight as she had banged her head very badly. She was a bit confused and kept talking about a snake in the house, so they wanted to keep an eye on her. They thought she was remembering a traumatic episode from her childhood.

"Who are you talking to?" her mother asked. "What's going on?"

"Nothing, Mum. Everything's all right."

Irene went back to the job in hand, caught the snake and took it out to the compost bin. As she returned to the kitchen she could hear the chimes of her mobile phone again.

"What's that noise?" called her mother. "What's going on?"

"Nothing, Mum. It's just my phone."

Irene could see that it was Don ringing.

"What is it?" she sighed.

"We've run out of toilet rolls," he said. "Did you get any?"

# The End of Eden

BARBARA EVANS

They sailed a ship to other lands,
And all the while they stayed in bands,
And groups to help to keep them safe,
Not knowing where the danger was.
And here lived Eve, still sweet and sinful.
And Adam of the palm tree land.

In Eden then, they found great wealth,
In graveyard caves beside the dead
In rocky tombs, on stony shelf
(And Eden's folk, still innocent,
Knew not the strangers' real intent.
The treasures were their talismans,
They marked a grieving sentiment
And not a treasure to be spent).

They took from them so easily.
Some of it they took by stealth,
By purchase and by sleight of hand.
Cajoling, swapping and by theft.
Then, necklace, crown and coronet,
They packed it off, in crate and chest.
They hauled it seaward 'cross the strand
On board the vessel near at hand.

And away they went upon the sea,
Upon the strange and foreign sea,
Where even the whales are different.
The wind was backing north and west.
Wildly licking force, course north,
Yes, north, north-west from Eden's Heaven.
And the coast was far and miles away.

It sank to the bottom of a foreign sea!
It sank, blank and tank to the bottom
Of a foreign sea of wondrousness.
At the very bottom every oaf fell,
And now lay tumbled with Davy Jones
(And often by the bar, things still wash up,
That once were Eden's treasures).

All that was Paradise, tidy in their funeral caves
Is now with weed and fish to dish and kiss, but all is gone...

Why take the treasure too soon, to lose it in the spume?
Spume and spout counts it for naught
When this loss was not meant to be,
Out there in the foamy sea.
It was for the ancestors,
It was for sweet Eden,
It was not anything
To do with them.

# *Things That Go Bump in the Night*

## LYNDA HOTCHKISS

"Nooooo! Not now, pleeeease!"

Avery Moss shouted to the heavens as raindrops began to fall on his bent back. To a casual passer-by, the words seemed to emanate from the ground itself, but in reality he was excavating unseen in an old brick pit. The rain started to fall heavily, and Moss was forced to climb out to take shelter under nearby trees.

He was a handsome man of some thirty-five years. Some would say he was a little eccentric as he favoured long straggly hair instead of the clipped and curled style favoured by men of the time. He also had a neatly clipped moustache and small goatee beard that finished in a point. In fact, he looked like a Royalist cavalier from the seventeenth century instead of the young poet and novelist of the early twentieth.

His line of work allowed him long lazy summers where he could look for inspiration for his next book, which would then be serialised in a weekly penny paper. It did not net him a great income, but he did not really worry too much about that, having inherited a small fortune from family members who had died childless. This year, he had chosen to spend the summer in rural Lincolnshire, and had taken the tenancy of a small cottage near the river in a backwater village off the beaten track. He enjoyed long walks along the riverbank and across fields where the growing crops waved in warm breezes. It was on one of those walks that he spotted a depression in the ground and chose it as a spot where he could eat his meagre lunch of bread, cheese and an apple. He had intended to partake of some ale at the local hostelry just round the bend in the river, but his attention was drawn to a pile of stones instead.

He held his hand out to see if the rain had stopped and harrumphed to find it getting heavier. He stamped his feet and leant against the tree once more. He would just have to wait.

This was the third day he had been clearing earth away from those stones. The first time he had simply used the toe and heel of his boot, dislodging very little in the way of dirt, due to the recent hot conditions that had baked everything. In fact, today's storm was most welcome to everybody complaining about the current heatwave, if somewhat inconvenient to his current labours. Yesterday he had returned bearing a small trowel and had managed to dig down about an inch all round before having to call it a day, due to his palms being covered with blisters from the tool handle. Today, he was better prepared, his sore hands bound with soft cloth. He toted a small spade, a pick, the same trowel, a stiff broom and a small soft brush, the type artists favoured. He carried them in an old sack and had made better progress since his early arrival, but everything was on hold while it rained.

Avery shuffled his feet, yawned, and sat down on the only dry patch under the large old chestnut tree where he had been standing for some twenty minutes. He took off his cloth hat and wiped his forehead with the back of his forearm. This removed the small dirty mark above his left eyebrow. He leaned his head back and closed his eyes.

When he opened them again, the rain had stopped and the sun was pushing its way through the dark clouds. The ground was wet and in places, there were small rushing rivulets of brown water making its uncertain way to the river. Avery got to his feet and rushed back to the old pit. The storm had aided his work, and there was a pool of water swirling in the hole he had made. He reached for the pick and hacked at the edges of the hole, finally allowing the muddy liquid to escape. When it had gone, he used his hands to remove the remaining dregs, and suddenly stopped.

"What the...?" he voiced as he stared at the strange shape that now appeared in the mud. His finger traced the outline of the artefact, and he began using the trowel to reveal what it was. It took about half an hour before he was able to lift out a long shape with bulbous ends. He walked down to the river, washed it and realised he had in his hands a bone, a long thick bone, probably an upper leg bone. He turned it this way and that, peering intently at it, and noting small notches on it in places. It seemed to be human. Carefully stowing it in his sack, he went back to his excavations. It took several hours but eventually his sack was crammed with strangely shaped muddy lumps. Hoisting it onto his back, Avery made his way home, intending to wash and examine his finds at home that very night.

Avery Moss worked till late cleaning each item, and placing it with care onto the large table in his kitchen. In fact, the table was one of only three pieces of furniture in the kitchen if you discounted the built-in range that provided heating and cooking facilities. The second was a large dresser in which pots and pans were stored, while several large mugs or jugs hung from hooks on a couple of shelves that supported a number of plates of various sizes and designs. A large earthenware jug held various items of cutlery and a big salver graced the very top, a salver much bedecked with grime and cobwebs. Moss rarely cooked and the salver, along with the rest of the kitchenware, had come with the property.

By eleven, all the finds were laid out and Avery stepped back to view his discovery. Although several bones were still missing, it was clearly a human skeleton, but the skull was far from human. He picked it up and looked at it more closely. Instead of the usual shape of a man's head, this skull was more elongated and the jaws projected outwards, something like a dog's.

"Incisors – six, seven, and the eighth is missing," he muttered. "Two canines at the top, and the same at the bottom. If I didn't know better, I would say this was the head of a large dog, something like the vicar's Irish wolfhound, or possibly a wolf."

He sat down on the third piece of furniture in the kitchen – a Windsor chair that needed careful use as he still needed to repair one of its legs that was slightly shorter than the others. He usually ensured the chair was placed in a certain spot where the floor's uneven surface compensated for the chair's wobble. From this spot, he stared at the skull for several minutes. He crossed and uncrossed his legs, rose from his seat and squatted at the table's edge, staring into the empty eye sockets until his eyes burned dry with looking. His knees ached from the bent position, and his feet grew cold. Avery finally stood erect and threw an old sheet over the assemblage of bones before heading upstairs. He closed the door to the stairs quietly, almost reverently, as if to honour the body laid on his kitchen table.

In his chamber, which was above the kitchen, he removed his boots and sat on the edge of a four-poster bed. He unfastened his watch from his waistcoat and placed it carefully on the nightstand next to his bed. He flicked open the watchcase, and smiled at the faded picture of his parents that he had fixed inside. He closed it with a snap, and lay on the bed, staring up at the canopy as his thoughts raced. *Could a man – or woman – have been buried out there in the old pit and then a dog, or wolf, ended up next to him?* he thought. *Or did the dog die first, and the human get buried on top? Were the bones just shovelled together and thrown there? Does anyone know who the man was, and why he was put in that particular spot? Did he just die there, unnoticed, or was he killed there? A work accident, or was it murder?*

Eventually, Avery Moss drifted off into a dream-haunted sleep.

Avery woke with a start. It was dark, but there was a full moon shining in through the small window, casting a shaft of silver light across the floor and the bed. He reached for his watch but his fumbling caused it to fall to the floor. Swinging his legs off the bed, he stopped in his tracks as a loud howl came from outside. In bare feet, he went to the window and looked out into the garden. His eyes took a minute or two to get accustomed to the night but he heard that ghastly howl again. It made his blood freeze but he did not turn away from the window. Suddenly, a movement caught his attention, and he was certain someone was skulking about in the shrubbery that marked the end of his garden.

He went to the bedroom door, and crept downstairs. The door at the bottom opened into the kitchen, and he opened it as carefully as he could. It creaked and squeaked, causing him to stop and hold his breath. The kitchen was also bathed in silky moonlight and the things on the table were highlighted at every lump and bump. Avery shivered and breathed out. His breath was white in the air. As he breathed out, a dark shadow passed the window, causing him to gasp.

He moved swiftly to the sink, holding it firmly for support as he peered outside. Suddenly, something rose up and looked back at him. In a split second he took in its glaring red eyes, hairy face and two large hands leaning on the glass.

There was an intense growl that became a howling, and an ear-splitting sound. Avery realised it was him screaming and backed away from the window, knocking into the table where his day's work lay spread out under a white pall. He could not move his eyes from the thing at the window. It lifted its hands, howled again, and thumped hard on the outside of the glass. It repeated this action several times, and eventually there was a splintering sound. A hand, or rather a large hairy paw, was thrust through the broken pane, grabbing at anything it could reach inside. Avery moved as quickly as he could to the stairs door, holding it open in case that thing came any nearer. His chest felt fit to burst as he held his breath. His heart was thudding so loudly he thought the beast might hear it. Then the window was empty, the moonlight streaming back in, and the thing was gone.

He relaxed and was about to step into the kitchen once more when he heard scratching. He turned his head to the back door, where the scratching was getting more frequent, and the howling started again.

Avery did not wait to see who or what came crashing through his door. He stepped up the stairs nimbly and silently, ensuring the door was latched and bolted from the inside. Nothing could get up the stairs now!

He was standing in the doorway of his chamber when he heard a loud crash. The back door had finally given way and whatever had been outside was now in his kitchen. The howling recommenced and went on for several minutes – or so it seemed. Each howl came from the heart, an anguished cry filled with sorrow. Avery started to feel a little pity for the creature that had broken into his home, but that sentiment did not last long. He soon realised that it was now trying to open the door to the stairs. He felt a cold sweat of terror come over him and he bolted into the chamber, closing and locking the door behind him. He spotted a large chest of drawers and dragged it from the left side of the room to block the door itself. Like the outside door, the door to the room where he slept opened inwards, so the heavy cabinet should stop the thing from entering. To make sure, he dragged a large dark wooden chest from the foot of his bed and lifted it, with great effort, until he was able to place it on top of the other piece of furniture. Sweating from his endeavours and from fear, he squatted at the end of his bed, watching the barricaded door intently. He was frozen with fear now; his only movement was to suddenly reach out and retrieve the fallen watch. He held it close to his chest, and prayed.

With a triumphant howl, the creature wrenched the door open, and now had access to the upper rooms. It carefully stepped up the stairs and sniffed the air. Another howl, and then it padded across the landing to the door that Avery had just barricaded. It reached out and twisted the bright shiny doorknob, but the door stayed shut. It turned and started to shove the door with its shoulder, but still the door stood firm against it. It tried every way it could to open the door, howling with rage every time it failed, while inside Avery shivered each time there was a thump.

Eventually, the concerted effort to come through the door stopped, and Avery listened hard to hear if it, the creature, had gone. He thought he could hear something padding up and down the landing, and he gripped the bedpost tighter, drawing his feet up onto the bed. He was terrified, and prayed the night would be over soon.

The padding outside the door stopped. Avery lifted his head, quietly slipped off the bed and listened at the door as closely as his barricade would let him. The thing had gone back down to the kitchen. He sighed with relief but was aware it might return to continue its assault on his room. He allowed himself to relax a little, and felt brave enough to glance out of the window. He looked down and saw two more creatures staring up at him – the same red eyes, the same hairy visage. They howled and were gone.

The howling started quietly at first, then there seemed to be more than one creature howling, as Avery identified different tones. Soon it was one cacophony of screeching, an unearthly screaming that chilled the marrow in the bones of God-fearing folk. Avery believed in God, but rarely attended church. He wished now that he had been more vigilant in his Christian obligations as a few words of comfort might be useful in this situation.

The howling stopped, and the crashing started. He could hear the smashing of plates and glass, the thudding and crashing as things were thrown around the kitchen. It went on for quite some time, and then the howling started again. When it stopped, he could distinctly hear footsteps outside his room once again. Whatever it was out there, it was mad as Hell, and had very little intention of going away.

He wasn't sure when he actually fell asleep but he woke up cold, cramped and hungry. The sun was shining in where the moonlight had been and all seemed quiet outside and inside the cottage. Stiffly, he went to the window and stared down on a garden that had flowers and vegetables uprooted or trampled, hedges pulled out and at least two of the fruit trees pushed over. He took down the makeshift barrier and cautiously opened the door. Nothing was there, and nothing was out of place, but a strong musky odour assailed his nostrils, making him wince slightly.

He crept down into the kitchen, where everything was wrecked. He heard his own sharp intake of breath as he viewed the scene of devastation – broken crockery, smashed windows. Clothing that had been drying on the high dryer had been ripped and thrown down on the floor, food supplies broken open and scattered across the same surface. Even the large dresser had been moved away from the wall and was tilted over, with its front resting on the edge of the range. The kitchen table that once held the meticulously laid-out skeleton was now on its back, three of its legs in the air and the fourth smouldering on the hearth. Only the wonky Windsor chair had escaped destruction, and on its seat, grinning at the cottage tenant, was the skull from the old brick pit. The bones that Avery had collected at the same time had been scattered around the room in a haphazard fashion that was at odds with the apparent reverence shown to the head.

Avery Moss took the stairs two at a time, and dressed quickly, checking his watch was firmly in his pocket. He gathered up the bones he had carefully cleaned the night before and placed them into a box that usually held potatoes while they germinated. Placing the skull on top, he grabbed his hat and went out. He didn't bother shutting the door. There was little left of the back door to close, and very little of value left intact inside. He strode purposefully to the place where his excavations still gaped raw and enticingly at him, but he had no intention, nor inclination, of continuing his work. He chose the spot where he felt he had unearthed the macabre items, and re-buried them as quickly but carefully as he could. He placed the stones back on the top in as close a fashion as he could recall. He then said a prayer over them, and hurried back home to clear the mess created overnight.

Avery Moss terminated his tenancy and hurried back to London. The locals spoke for many years of the time when the howling seemed to go on all night and of the nice young man who left the village far sooner than he had intended when he rented the old cottage down by the river. No one local ever wanted to live there, however desperate they might be, as it had been for as long as they could remember, and no one local ever tried to use Old Brick Pit Field for anything but growing grass. They never let their animals graze there for more than a few hours, and they certainly would not frequent the area at night. There were too many things that went bump in the night!

# *Summer 1963*

### PETER CORRIN

Evaluating memorable holidays from the past can throw up all too many anomalies as one tries to compare unlikes. How I felt at different ages, how the journey affected me, who I met on the holiday, what I saw, what I learned, what the weather was like: all the myriad details that go to make an experience and to make it dwell in the mind. If you add in the focus and magnification effect of remembering over a number of years, it is all too easy to get a distorted view of the past. I revisited a number of photograph albums to try to get the right type of inspiration and one year sprang to the forefront – 1963, the year of transformation and, horrifyingly, fifty years ago.

I was eleven in May 1963 and at a boarding prep school, which tried my patience beyond belief. I was growing very quickly and was to reach 6 ft in height that June! Blessedly, I had been deemed to be unfit for normal sports, like cricket, and was put with the odd-job man, Harry, to help him in maintaining the school grounds instead. This meant that at eleven years of age I was being taught how to handle a big, recalcitrant motor mower and a very cantankerous vintage Fordson tractor, how to creosote the wooden fence around the swimming pool and how to manage an Allen motor scythe in the cricket outfield. Trust me, this was brilliant from my point of view and meant that I could strip to the waist like Harry all summer long and also use my large, developing physique to do something useful.

By the end of the summer term, in July, I was bronzed, fit and tall! My parents announced that they had selected northern Italy for the family holiday that year and had rented a villa in a little town called Laigueglia, a few miles south of Alassio. Out came the family atlas and we soon tracked where we were going to. I was most fortunate to have parents who were willing, and able, to go beyond the norm for holidays, but this was a great excitement, as this was the first foray on to the Continent!

In the whirlwind of getting everything ready for the due date, my mind has let a lot of the detail slip, but I can recall packing my suitcase with all the necessaries to meet my expectations, including two new, modern swimming costumes that actually fitted – even when wet – and did not drag or sag or hold a couple of pints of water when you came out of the sea! I have no doubt that I was also equipped with what other clothing my mother thought I should have with me!

When the day came around, I helped lug the suitcases down stairs, collected together all the loose items as well, and helped to stow everything in the boot of Dad's Wolseley 6/110. The pre-holiday checklist was brought out and each relevant item was ticked off – my dad was nothing if not methodical!

And so we set off from the Midlands, bound for Dover and a ferry to a great adventure. As ever, I was in the front passenger seat because I was a lousy traveller and would only be ill otherwise, and because I was the only one who could reliably read maps. My sister and mother occupied the back seat with my sister's nose in a book and my mum gazing as the scenery sped past, or snoozing.

The excitement of the ferry port with all the smells and sounds was intoxicating for an eleven-year-old; the combined smells of the sea and the diesel were very heady and, after the regulation queue, we were guided onto the vast ship and into a parking space. Having secured the vehicle for the trip to France, we were herded by Dad up into the ship proper and then did the tourist thing of looking at the duty free, then for something to eat, and finally we went outside onto the deck for some air and for the view. The day was reasonably calm and the gentle swell inside the harbour did nothing to upset any of us, though we had all been issued with anti-seasickness pills by Mum before even getting on board. Soon the ship was under way and sure enough the swell increased slightly as we left the harbour and set out on the Channel, but only Mum showed signs of being affected and the rest of us strolled around as we began to appreciate the history of where we were and to enjoy the splendour of the white cliffs as they slowly receded behind us.

In next to no time we were requested by the tannoy to go back down to the car to get ready to disembark. We had watched the French coast get closer and seen the port of Calais with its legendary clock tower, and now it was time to actually touch a foreign country. Dad eased the car up the ramp and back onto dry land, much to the relief of my mother, and then we did the Customs thing and finally drove out of the port area, destination a short way off at Boulogne.

First off, Dad found us a restaurant to fill up in and we witnessed his execrable French, as he tried to order! He also found a peculiar method of getting attention by raising a forefinger and saying "Garkon!" loudly, which seemed to bemuse the very attractive, teenaged waitress, and remained a family legend for the rest of his life!

Fed and watered, we proceeded at a leisurely pace to Boulogne, where we navigated the town to reach the railway station for the start of the next adventure – the overnight Wagon-Lits train down the spine of France to Lyon. The family had to get out of the car with our overnight kit and wait whilst Dad drove the car off, under instruction from an official, to get it loaded onto the transporter wagons at the back of the train. Then, when he reappeared, we went to find our compartments for the night, Mum with sister and Dad with me, and get used to the layout of the train. It was not really Orient Express quality but the polished wood of the corridor coaches was very impressive and the dining car, when we got there, was very smart. The fold-out bunk-type beds were very comfortable and, once you got used to the sway of the train and the noise of crossings and stations, it was all too easy to sleep away the excitement of the day.

The next morning came too early, a six o'clock start with breakfast in the dining car at seven and then the procedure to get the car off the train and get us packed back in. We were soon under way, after a long check of the map, and I navigated us out of Lyon towards the south-east and Chambery, heading for the Alps and the then-inevitable climb over the mountains to cross into Italy – remember this was many years before the modern tunnels were bored.

French countryside did not look all that different from England as we sped along; just the miles of poplar trees marking the roads as foreign and, of course, seeing all of it from the 'wrong' side of the road. I watched the traffic and the peculiar vehicles which the French seemed to like, most of which I had never seen before. Citroëns, Renaults, Panhards, Peugeots and Fiats seemed to be the standard fare and hardly anything that I was used to like Austins, Morrises, Fords and so on. It all added even more to the exotic excitement of the adventure.

Once we hit the hills and the winding, bend-ridden roads up them, our average speed began to drop. Whilst Dad and I enjoyed the spectacular scenery as we approached the Mont Cenis pass, it was obvious that it was tiring driving and the complaints from the back seats of ears 'popping' were not so much fun!

Eventually there came a call from the rear that a 'natural break' was needed and by this time we were driving in cloud, so spotting a suitable place was not so easy. I saw a sign saying that there was a layby a kilometre ahead and that was agreed to be acceptable, only when we got there the cloud was all around us and there was snow outside! Legs were duly stretched and comfort was obtained to a female chorus of it being cold... a flask of tea was produced and sandwiches too, and then on we went to the Customs post letting us in to Italy.

We had to wait a while to get through this post, and a certain eleven-year-old spent quite a while falling in love with a long, sleek, exotic, red Ferrari. Then the owner returned to it, started it up and made the same eleven-year-old ecstatic with a sound like nothing on Earth – it was like finding Dan Dare's spaceship on the bleak mountainside!

Rolling again, the North Italian roads were soon bathed in sunshine and it seemed as though the roads were less bendy, though, going downhill, Dad was being very careful not to use his brakes too much, so progress was still a bit stately. We were headed for the Torino bypass system and managed to navigate it quite well as we pushed on through the late afternoon towards the Mediterranean. We reached the sea at Savona and turned south for Alassio and our eventual destination of Laigueglia, but there was a slight fly in the joy of being so close to our destination: we had no detailed map to find the actual villa we were supposed to be staying in and the tiredness was beginning to make the whole atmosphere in the car just a bit irritable, certainly in the back seat! Dad drove on into the twilight, as we continued to gaze at the sea and think about just how far from home we were.

The road sign said Laigueglia. Now all we had to do was find where we were supposed to go. I got the phrasebook out and Dad selected a suitable target for his first Italian discussion, pulled the car over and wound down the window... "Scusi," he started, "por favori, Villa Traviata?"

The man looked at Dad thoughtfully and then said, "You're English, aren't you?"

You could have knocked Dad down with a sneeze, the one person he picks out on the street in Italy and they are English! Not only that but, beyond belief, he did know where the villa was and how to get there! I strongly believe that my dad always had a really effective guardian angel, because every time he really winged it, he came up trumps! The chap gave us detailed directions and off we went, up into a tight, twisty lane to the right, then left at the fork and second on the left.

Bingo! We had arrived! As we pulled up I noticed that there was an English Humber parked outside the neighbouring villa and that it too had an English number plate, and a Northamptonshire one at that; even then I was a known 'motor anorak'. Talk about coincidence! Then the chap from that villa came walking over towards our car with some keys and said, "Hello, Jack," to my dad, "I didn't know that you were coming here too." It was a man and his family from a few doors up the road at home: a fellow councillor, a fellow accountant and one of Dad's golfing friends. My mum has never believed that it was not a put-up job, but I think that they had really just not compared notes. It was a really 'homely' start to a great holiday, but Dad always compared notes with friends about where they would be going on holiday, and when, after that.

# Try Something New

### BRIAN HUMPHREYS

Heaven could not be much better than this, thought Tommy Higgins, as he leaned into the early morning wind, his running shoes crunching leaves and twigs with every stride, his tracksuit clinging to his body as he reached the final turn. The early morning sun rose in the south, chasing away the early frost, the smell of damp woodland filled his senses and the trees, swaying in the wind, seemed to wave him goodbye as he reached the clearing, just short of the isolated cottage in which he hoped to begin his masterpiece.

Tommy was an author and a creature of habit. An early morning run, a shower and then a raw egg was his routine preparation before facing the blank, intimidating pages of his A4 notebook, not that he was short of ideas; he was in a rich grain of creativity, including a new book to be called *Try Something New*. He hoped that it would help not only him, but others who were creatures of habit. Change was a good thing, he had decided; it could stimulate new creativity and growth in a person.

Tommy left the woods in his wake and powered up the slight incline to the cottage, his sweat-covered eyes almost missing the container of eggs nestled in the grass verge. He skidded to a halt, took a breath, and retraced his steps. Three large eggs had been placed in a basket with a barely legible note: *FREE EGGS*. Who could have left them? There was no cottage for miles around, and nobody knew he was there, except for the anonymous online booking agent. Correction, he thought, gasping for breath, someone knew.

Tommy was a city boy, used to medium-sized brown eggs in a plastic egg box from the supermarket. 'Always check to see if any are cracked,' his mother taught him. 'It's no good finding out when you get home.' But these were not supermarket eggs; they were huge. Duck eggs perhaps, or pheasant eggs? Which game birds were common in Cornwall? He hadn't a clue. He picked up a large egg. Emus perhaps? These large eggs were not part of his routine. His routine food, including medium-sized brown supermarket eggs, lay on the kitchen floor in a box, waiting to be stored.

It would be rude to refuse this anonymous gift, he reasoned, and in any case, how could he write about *Trying Something New* if he wasn't prepared to do so himself?

He chose the middle egg and lifted it head-high. The shell was a strange mottled brown and cream colour. 'Come on, eat your eggs, they're full of goodness and will make you strong,' his mother always told him.

His fingernails began to crack the shell; he tilted his head back as he lifted the egg over his mouth. For a second, the egg blotted out the morning sun, becoming almost transparent, and for a micro-second, the embryo inside seemed to move as he opened the shell and let the contents pour into his open mouth. The smell was putrid like mouldy cheese, and it took three almighty swallows for the contents to pass down his throat. He gagged violently like a celebrity in the Australian jungle, but Ant and Dec were nowhere to be seen.

He grabbed his water bottle, gulping down copious amounts of water in an effort to remove the vile taste from his mouth. If that's what duck eggs taste like, you can keep 'em. His stomach did not take kindly to the invasion of foreign matter and all was not well with his insides.

He heard a strange howling noise from inside the woods, the sun dipped low behind distant clouds and the wind freshened as he carried the other large eggs into the kitchen of the cottage, placing them on the draining board.

Doubled up with pain, he staggered and fell onto the old settee. He suddenly wished that he was back in the comfort of his own home with Anna; at least she would know what to do.

Like the weather, his happiness deteriorated rapidly. He grabbed his notepad and sketched an outline of the morning's events, before lapsing into a long, haunted sleep.

He woke in unfamiliar surroundings, the dark clouds outside providing a gloomy atmosphere. The pains in his stomach quickly reminded him of his situation. He scanned the dusty interior of the old run-down cottage; the laughing cavalier picture over the open fireplace seemed to mock his predicament. He could barely move. He felt weak and in the grip of food poisoning or a stomach bug. In the shaft of light coming through the open kitchen door, he wrote a few more notes before drifting out of consciousness.

The instant-replay of the moving embryo inside the eggshell caused him to wake with a start. Racked with stomach pains, he longed for his noisy children. Noise would be a good thing right now; it would take his mind off this nightmare situation.

He could feel his strength draining away minute-by-minute and his regular stomach pains were now accompanied by hot flushes. He would not make it to the front door, never mind his car, and the cottage, deliberately chosen for its isolation, had no phone. Until this thing passed, he knew he was going nowhere, but he desperately needed water.

He lowered himself to the floor and inched across the room until the food box was within reach. His stomach seemed to grow with every pull, and pain intensified as he dragged the box back to the settee. Springs groaned once again, as he slumped back onto the settee. He slaked his thirst, the cold water cooling him a little. He grabbed his notepad and wrote down some more thoughts before lapsing into another horrific embryo-movement nightmare.

Tommy woke in severe pain, gasping for breath. He removed his tracksuit top and T-shirt to combat the increasing hot flushes. This stomach bug was a nightmare of his own making. He had placed himself in the middle of nowhere to awaken his inner self, and he had swallowed the raw egg. There was no one to blame but himself. He drank the last of his water; his stomach was huge now, and the water seemed to slosh around inside him, giving a sense of movement.

If only I wrote horror stories, he thought, this one would be a cracker. He pictured the scene from the film *Alien* when a strange creature burst out of John Hurt's stomach. He stifled a laugh, causing another bout of pain. *Am I going insane?* He wrote down his thoughts before feeling around his ever-enlarging stomach. Was that a movement? Was that a kick?

His dreams were becoming more vivid and bizarre. How could a man possibly become pregnant, let alone with an alien's child?

As he woke, the eerie silence was shattered by a large egg falling onto the kitchen floor. Purple liquid seeped out and as the crack widened, a scaly withered dead hand flopped into view, releasing the now-familiar putrid smell. Tommy vomited over the side of the settee, purple and orange mucus stringing from his mouth. He grabbed his pen and scribbled, *I have an alien growing inside me.*

Having just given birth to E.T. in another nightmare, he woke to find the room different somehow. Then he saw them: two hooded figures occupying the armchairs. A low, resonating, guttural voice whispered, 'Don't be alarmed, it's not good for you or junior.'

Instinctively, Tommy grabbed his stomach. There was definite movement inside. In the poorly lit room, he could not see the hooded figures clearly.

'Why me; why not a female jogger?'

'That's a good question, but first please take a drink; it will ease your pain.'

Tommy eyed the strange vessel beside him.

'I can assure you, it doesn't taste as bad as our placenta. Go on, try something new.'

Tommy drank the lukewarm liquid, his pain eased quickly and the thing inside him calmed down.

'You are thinking of birth only in human terms by the female of your species. Understandable, considering the situation.'

Tommy watched in horror as a thick red line slowly zig-zagged down his chest and over his swollen stomach, as if drawn by an invisible marker, and the movement inside increased.

'You are *still* thinking in human terms and wondering how long to delivery. It won't be long now. Your nine-month gestation period is just one of the many failings of the human race. Please, take another drink.'

Needing more pain relief, Tommy did so. 'Human babies feed on nutrients from their mother, so what is junior feeding on?'

From the darkness beneath the hood, a strange voice replied: 'Just like a human baby will instinctively locate a nipple, so junior will have latched onto a blood vessel. Human blood has a lot going for it: temperature regulation, an immune system, the distribution of oxygen. Obviously the human body fails at everything else, like walking upright. Whose stupid idea was that? All that pressure on two feet, two ankles, two knees and two hips. But human blood, now that might prove to be the answer.'

'You mean I'm just an experiment?'

'On the contrary, think of yourself as a pioneer, and if your notes are good enough, you could become more famous than Dr Christiaan Barnard; posthumously, of course. Please take another drink. Junior wants to come out and play.'

Tommy finished the last of the anaesthetic and watched in horror as the red jagged line down his body began to open. 'But how did you know that I'd eat the raw egg?'

'We put the thought in your head. I must congratulate you on your swallowing technique.' The hooded figure then passed Tommy his notepad. 'Would you like to record your last thoughts?'

As Tommy scribbled his last words, his rib-cage cracked open. Purple juice came first, followed quickly by the familiar putrid smell as purple fingers emerged, tearing his flesh apart.

A low, resonating, guttural voice shouted louder and louder, 'It's a boy, it's a boy!'

Semi-conscious, and with tear-filled eyes, Tommy was paralysed with fear. Hands were shaking his shoulders and with the last of his strength, he fought desperately to shake them off.

'It's a boy, it's a boy,' said a deep melodic voice in a Welsh accent. *A Welsh accent?*

Tommy opened one eye. Shaking his shoulders was Nurse Bronwyn, and he was in the maternity hospital waiting room.

'It's a boy, Mr Higgins, and your wife and baby are doing fine. Would you like to see them now?'

*'It was all a dream' is a criminal way to end a short story and I apologise. The truth is that this actually happened to me! I did fall asleep in the waiting room, my wife did give birth to a boy, and every now and again, my son does behave like an alien.*

# *Albert*

## JENNY MURPHY

Albert would have loved his funeral and laughed his socks off at my dilemma. It even surpassed the time I had to prise a client off a coffin after she had prostrated herself over the wobbly stand. This was, of course, immediately after she discovered she had been left some items in the will.

At all times, Albert said what he wanted and acted as he chose. As a prisoner of war, he had seen it all and worked hard at developing his eccentricities. Neighbours who were less than civil saw their gardens wilt overnight, victims of his massive stash of Weedol. Doris, his long-suffering wife, bore the brunt of his tongue as he berated her with tough love.

I saw him a few days before his death, and was coerced into pushing him outside the hospital for a cigarette, which he could hardly hold, never mind puff on. Despite being on dialysis, he was frequently moved to the dementia ward as doctors failed to recognise his sense of humour, and then, suddenly, he was gone.

I allowed plenty of time for the journey to the crematorium, as my knowledge of the Leeds traffic system was poor. At the third attempt, I made it around the island and through the crematorium gates. There was just one problem: my foot went flat to the floor as all brakes failed. The funeral party scattered, leaping swiftly aside in their confusion, as, shaking, I pumped the brake in a vain hope of some response. The only way to stop was to execute a handbrake turn worthy of a car chase in a James Bond movie.

I saw Albert's coffin arrive to my left, and managed to climb out of the car in a suitably dignified fashion to join the rest of the mourners.

The vicar spoke glowingly of a person who could not in my wildest imagination have been Albert, while I plotted a route home that did not necessitate going down a hill. Decorum dictated that I could not call the AA pick-up truck to the crematorium; neither could I push my car around the corner across three lanes of traffic in search of a garage.

The journey home took several hours and gave me plenty of time to reflect on the life and loss of dear old Albert. As I remembered Albert's wicked grin, I could almost see the coffin rocking with laughter.

# The Farm

## BARBARA EVANS

The orange orb of the sun is balanced quivering on the tightrope thread of the horizon. It scintillates around its irregular wavering perimeter like a vacant halo. It looks like molten metal, a red-hot ember or Hell's distant open mouth, but soon it has slipped and sunk into a semisphere.

Gilded by its glow, the rambling leafless hawthorn hedge forms fantastic figures. The sinister silhouette shapes conjure dark serpents to the mind's eye, or a creeping coven of crooked witches. Beyond this tracery of trees, the land slopes sharply down a steep decline and slides into the sand and sea at its foot. The fallow meadow's wind-combed, silken gold-green locks lie flat and smooth over the slope disrupted here and there into a hummock.

At the foot of the slope stand the good cattle, patient and plodding, eating and waiting. Waiting willingly for a milking, waiting for the farmer. The farmer who will lead them, tie them, tell them, help them, heal them. The farmer is the centre of their world. He is their feeder, their father, and their friend. He is their god, their giver, their government. They live encompassed by his will, they will die at his command. The sea whispers a warning. It knows the fate of cattle.

Stained by the slow sunset, the flowery garden glows in its light. Its colours are washed over in shades of flame. Pink, peach and purple are all painted in ruddy colours. A low stone wall ties the garden to the little house as if by its apron strings. Whole and wholesome, the flowers enclosed within its stony embrace issue from this restraint like steam from a cooking pot; they burst beyond its boundaries.

Bunched abundant blood-red roses hang out over the lane, hindering the unwary. Fat clumps of hydrangea make great swelling heaps, rising and spreading like loaves. Wisteria wanders roof-high and wayward; its delicious amethyst, grape-like clusters hang like suspended drops of damson wine. Heaped on the wall, the sweet-smelling humming honeysuckle hides the lairs of birds and small beasts. Crowded crimson clematis crawls, creeps, and clambers over the stones and up into the tree. It is bunched on the branches of the single rowan, and massed there like many fat cats sleeping in its arms. In every bare space a vine hangs out her wine-red damasks to air, in interleafing rows. Every growing thing is filled with the will to wander. The blossoms bubble, froth, and flow over the stone perimeter, like a pan boiling over. They look as if they would wander like a slow river, down the far-reaching fields to the ocean, and not stop there, but wash all over the globe!

Behind the house, the big barn towers tall and cavernous. Inside, the hay is high-piled in heaps of plenty. It rises in steps and soft mounds up into the roof. The top-most hay is hidden from view under the sagging moss and lichen-lidded roof. It is a secret place. Under this roof is a hidden bower, and here lies Sally, empty of all but love.

# *Hands On*

## SALLY ANN NIXON

We have just put it away for another year. Every year now for twenty-five years – a quarter of a century, a catch in the throat or the blink of an eye. My son's hands heft the large plastic box into the attic, whilst I fidget about on the landing offering advice and caution. Our roles have been reversed for some time now. He thinks that I am unsafe on the ladder and he is probably right. I watch his hands, a man's hands, slightly battle-scarred, grubby, capable. The plastic box is stashed away.

Twenty-five years ago, he was tiny, my son. Fair, foursquare, stubby and determined. A three-year-old dynamo. We had been to his sister's nativity play – she was an angel – and he was pensive as I drove home through the lights and Christmas traffic.

"We have to welcome that baby into our home, Mum. That angel said so."

I smiled vaguely, concentrating on the traffic.

"We don't have a crib or anything for a little baby."

He looked at the picture on the front of the school's Christmas programme.

"Mum. We don't have a stable for him and he's only little. He'll get all wet and muddy and cold."

My son was distressed. I said all the things that mothers say to distract and comfort, handing out warm chocolate and Christmas buns when we arrived home. My daughter needed help to get out of her halo and wings. My son, frowning, pulled on his wellies and stomped off into the garden.

It was getting dark, so I switched on the Christmas lights, put baked potatoes and casserole to heat through in the oven and called both children in to watch *The Wind in the Willows*. Outside, the evening began to freeze.

My small son staggered in, covered in sawdust and smelling of wood shavings and cold. He was burdened with many, many offcuts from the woodpile in the shed, with a random collection of nails, screws and small woodworking tools sticking out of his duffle coat pockets. Thick cobwebs clung to his sleeves and hair.

Red-cheeked and triumphant, he dropped the wood onto the kitchen floor. Spiders and splinters scattered everywhere.

"I make that baby a stable," he announced. "Look!"

And he began to fit the offcuts together into a rough rectangle, three sides and a roof, standing on a flattish base with a small circle of wood to go inside the stable, to keep the baby dry and safe up out of the mud.

So that is what we did. The potatoes baked, the casserole bubbled and together the three of us glued and nailed and screwed together a rough shelter. My daughter fetched straw from her rabbit's supply. She stuck it to the stable roof and tucked it into the tiny stable taking shape on the kitchen table. We sprayed it with canned snow and decorated it with sprigs of ivy and holly from the hedgerow. And there it was. A place to welcome the baby.

My son clasped his pudgy, scratched little hands, just as grubby and dusty as today.

"We did it, Mum. On Christmas night that baby will come with Father Christmas and have a place with us to stay."

And so our very own family nativity has been there for the baby for every Christmas since. Who am I to argue with such loving theology?

# Crème de la Crème

## VICTORIA HELEN TURNER

### A COMEDY SKETCH

The action takes place in the village of Little-Mousing-in-the-Marsh

### CHARACTERS

**Delilah**  A snobbish Siamese cat, belonging to Lord and Lady Nohall, at the Manor House

**Tabitha**  Slightly timid tabby cat friend of Delilah, belonging to Mrs Toogood, the vicar's wife

**Aurora**  A bragging Persian cat, belonging to Mr and Mrs Woodbee

**Thomasina**  A ginger cat, friend of Aurora, belonging to Miss Rosy Parker, the post mistress

SCENE: The Village Green

*Two pairs of cats are sitting on opposite sides of the green, basking in the morning sun.*

**Delilah** *(with a sniff, waving to Aurora and Thomasina)*
Morning, ladies. Lovely day.

**Aurora/Thomasina**  Morning.

**Delilah** *(to Tabitha)*  Silly cat! Thinks she's the crème de la crème, just because her humans, the Woodbees, have built that great ugly house. My fiancée Thomas says it's jerry-built, and he should know, his human's a builder.

**Tabitha**  I think your Tom's a real brick, Delilah.

**Delilah** *(to Tabitha)*  I heard the other day that Mr Woodbee has been made an EMM PEE and he's going somewhere called 'The House of Commons'. Well, he should be all right; he's common enough, and whatever an EMM PEE is, he must be qualified for it, at least the second half!

**Tabitha** *(naively)*  In what way?

**Delilah**  Well, as it happens, on Saturday nights, when Tom and I are, er... gazing at the moonlight; you know, singing love songs from our favourite musical, *CATS*, well, I've seen old Woodbee come out of the Cat and Fiddle and go to the other side of the hedge, so if his performance at this 'House of Commons' is anything like the one behind the hedge, he should make an excellent EMM PEE!

**Tabitha** *(chuckling)*  Oh – I get you. Does your Tom ever help his human builder in his work?

**Delilah**  Hmm – he tries to – but *if* he tries, Mr Builder just shouts at him and says, "Tom's just caterwauling!"

**Tabitha**  Mmm – humans are funny sometimes, aren't they? *(They both yawn)*

**Delilah**  I don't know about you, but I'm going to take a cat nap.

**Tabitha**  Meee – tooo. *(They gradually fall asleep)*

**Aurora**  Look at those two, lazy cats, asleep in the middle of the morning.

**Thomasina**    Between you and me, Aurora *(looking to the left, right, and behind)*, I heard my mistress, Miss Rosy Parker, telling her friend the butcher lady something very interesting.

**Aurora** *(eagerly)*    Do tell.

**Thomasina**    Apparently, when daft old Delilah's Lady Nohall goes up to London on Wednesdays, and Mr Toogood the vicar visits the bishop on the same day, Mrs Toogood calls on Lord Nohall – know what I mean?

**Aurora**    Oh, I do! I do!

**Thomasina**    And that's not all.

**Aurora**    You mean there's more?

**Thomasina** *(nodding)* The funny thing is that my boyfriend, who lives at the pub 'The Queen's Paws' in the next village, has seen the vicar (in ordinary clothes, of course) and Lady Nohall register for a room in the name of Mr and Mrs Smith. Very original, don't you think?

*(They both fall about laughing)*

**Aurora**    I bet that stuck-up cat Delilah doesn't know a thing about it, and old Tabitha's too dumb!

**Thomasina**    I bet Tabitha thinks Mrs Toogood is going on an errand of mercy to Lord Nohall.

**Aurora**    Well, she probably is, if he's married to old Lady Nohall. She's got a face like the back of the village bus.

| | |
|---|---|
| **Thomasina** | It's probably Mrs Toogood's good deed for the day, while the vicar is giving spiritual consolation to her ladyship. |
| **Aurora** | Well, the spiritual bit comes out of a bottle, while he demonstrates the sins of the flesh. I know, because Jaws, my boyfriend, peers through the bedroom window! |

*(They both fall about laughing, again)*

*Aurora and Thomasina gradually stop laughing and begin to yawn. Like the other two, they nod off – while Delilah and Tabitha wake up and stretch.*

| | |
|---|---|
| **Delilah** | Look at her – Aurora, silly old mew, and that gas bag Thomasina. They've dropped off! Worn out by gossiping, I suppose! |
| **Tabitha** | Yes, Thomasina's a terrible gossip, just like her human, Miss Rosy Parker. Do you know, I've seen the living quarters over the post office? There's no room to swing a cat! |
| **Delilah** *(smiling)* | There may be no room to swing a cat, but another kind of swinging goes on there. |
| **Tabitha** | What do you mean? |
| **Delilah** | Well *(looking to the left, right, and behind)*, Mr Builder did something to the roof of the post office and my Thomas went to inspect the work afterwards, and what do you think he saw through Rosy Parker's bedroom window? |
| **Tabitha** | I've no idea, do tell. |

| | |
|---|---|
| **Delilah** *(winking)* | He saw old Woodbee and Rosy Parker, and they were... well, the only connection with the post office – as to their activity, I mean – was Postman's Knock – know what I mean? |
| **Tabitha** | Disgusting! *(Covers her mouth with a paw)* |
| **Delilah** | And that's not all! While Woodbee is at the post office... well, I shouldn't think even that stupid Aurora drinks ten pints of cream a week – but the milkman delivers it all right, straight to Mrs Woodbee when her old man's out, and she must have an enormous bill to pay, because the milkman's always there at least two hours – know what I mean? *(Digs Tabitha in the ribs with a paw)* |
| **Tabitha** | Disgusting! |
| **Delilah** | And the funny thing is, old Woodbee always goes home drunk – from the pub and the PO – and he daren't wake up his wife, and he also forgets his key every time, and that stupid Aurora sleeps in the hall at night. I know, because Tom and I peer through the side window. Do you know what old Woodbee does? |
| **Tabitha** | No. |
| **Delilah** | He looks through the letterbox at daft Aurora – and then he whispers, "Pssst, puss, let me in." And do you know what Aurora replies? "ME... OW!" |

CURTAIN

# My Prize Pumpkin

## BARBARA EVANS

Three stone is what my pumpkin weighs
And it is sure to win the day.
Can hardly lift it from the earth.
The challenge is "the greatest girth".

Can't lift it in the car away,
So barrow goes and car must stay
And I must push for all I'm worth
To try it out for greatest girth.

My pumpkin was a little thing.
It crept right through a trellis hole.
It grew and grew till it was king
And showing it became my goal.

Then I find I beat the rest!
A pound and fifty is my prize.
But what of all this is best:
I get a cup of middle size!

Off I go with my wheelbarrow.
The barrow, it is pumpkin-size.
Wheeling through the churchyard narrow
Did you see me with my prize?

# Welsh Retreat
# 2014

### SALLY ANN NIXON

We have been learning to accept the dark.
To accept it as a friend and not to fear it.
To welcome its embrace and find its comfort.
To be at one with the dark and return to stillness and peace.

This place aids such a meditation.
It stands, grey, compact and alone in the valley,
Overlooking the shifting, clouded lake, hills behind, beside,
Before, sacred for millennia with the vast sky.

It is autumn, late, crisp days, with cool and starry nights.
The dawn brings mist, cloaking the lake,
Blurring the hills and wraiths dance over the water,
Pine cones nest on the ground and water birds drift placid, unafraid.

We are on retreat and we are in silence.
Much gesturing at mealtimes –
The humour of request, thanks and apology.
Gradually our vision opens and our senses wake.

We learn, we pray in rhythm in the semi-twilight darkness.
Outside the Welsh rain falls.
A lilting wind nudges the trees and lifts the fallen leaves.
It smells of nearly winter and the prick of ice.

But this is all part of the quiet of this place.
A squirrel gathering outside the window
Counterpoints the ritual of the priest,
As he leads the midday chapel prayer.

It is the last day and I walk about the garden.
A robin greets me, sleek, expectant as I slip him breakfast crumbs.
A watery sun shivers across the lake and the leaves shine.
All co-exists in deep serenity.

# *Home Truths*

GUY JENKINSON

"What the blazes have you done to *my* planet?"

The shouted question crashed through my sleeping mind. The stentorian baritone I might have ignored, but I defy anyone to sleep through fanfares of golden trumpets plus a blaze of light resembling sunrise seen from a range of eight feet.

Terrified into wakefulness, I shot bolt-upright – cricking my back in the process. Attempting to focus on the imposing figure standing at the foot of the bed, I uttered the pitifully unoriginal, "Who are you?"

"I am the owner's representative, and the duly appointed agent for this planet." The clarion reply had an almost choral quality that left majestic echoes hanging in the air, whilst the light intensity softened to a medium-dazzle.

The after-images slowly cleared from my vision and I saw the speaker, robed in shimmering white that matched his outspread wings... *wings?* Stunned, I blurted, "You look just like an—"

"—an angel," he interrupted, tiredly. "Very well, if you prefer: I am an Emissary of the Almighty. The title 'Angel' is an accurate, if somewhat obsolescent, designation."

He pointed an accusatory finger at me. "I repeat, just what have you bunch of pillocks *done* to this planet?"

My tongue felt like the inside of an old trainer as I croaked, "I don't understand the question... whoever you are." Still dopey from my interrupted slumber, I stared at him blankly: 'like a stunned mullet', as our Australian cousins so graphically put it.

The angel sighed. "My name is Michael and, to assist your understanding, let me put the question into context by starting with a few home truths: as I understand it, for twenty centuries this planet has seen widespread poverty, famines, pandemics, slavery, wars, pollution and self-inflicted ecological disasters. Two recent conflicts were global and, so far, whilst you have barely avoided a full-scale thermonuclear exchange, you still remain at risk from nuclear, chemical and biological weapons." Michael folded his impressive wings into an "at-ease" position and sat down on the end of the bed. "You endure rampant crime, widespread terrorism, petty sectarian conflicts and vicious tribal squabbles. As for your centres of population: dozens of your cities exist for no apparent purpose except to act as breeding sites – every year, millions are born into hopeless poverty."

He paused for breath, so I thought it opportune to attempt some reply. However, even as I opened my mouth Michael pre-empted any response with, "Shut up and listen!" before continuing his harangue: "Famine, disease, war, crime, and environmental pollution... mostly attributable to uncontrolled overpopulation." In tones dripping with sarcasm he asked, "Did I omit anything? Oh, yes... the insignificant matter of an imminent collapse of the planet's entire biosphere!"

I struggled to assemble my thoughts as Michael averted his eyes upwards, apparently addressing an unseen entity: "I've been away for only a few millennia – now just look at the state of the place... why me?" Fixing me with a piercing gaze, he snarled, "NOW do you understand the question?"

"Why ask me?" I protested, somewhat taken aback by the tirade of accusation. "I don't represent humanity – I'm just a county councillor. Why not dump this on the Prime Minister or the American President... even the United Nations?"

"Don't worry," said Michael, 'that's already been taken care of, but, in addition to that, tonight we are visiting *every* person who is now, or soon will be, in a position of authority or influence. Twenty years from now you will be" – Michael broke off and chuckled – "one of those people... but I can't tell you any more than that."

Recovering my composure I decided to enter more into the spirit of the debate. Tongue-in-cheek I asked, "What about Genesis 1:28, '*Be*

*fruitful, multiply, and replenish the Earth'* – isn't that Holy Writ?"
OK, it was a rather silly jibe; in any case, I agreed with Michael about
population growth and, offhand, I honestly could think of nothing to
say in defence of mankind's abysmal stewardship of the planet.

Michael snorted. "Quoted out of context! In any case *'replenish'*
means restock, *not* to increase indefinitely, to the detriment of all other
species! Didn't you dimwits ever think that doubling the planet's
population every seventy years was just a tad profligate?" He gestured
towards the Bible in the bedside bookcase and sneered, as if
addressing a backward child, "You're not supposed to take it *literally*
– it's *allegorical*. You surely can't believe that the entire Cosmos was
created in just seven times twenty-four hours, do you? It's a
metaphor: seven aeons of development over billions of years." He
struck his forehead with the heel of his hand and muttered, "I knew I
was right to argue against relying on primates instead of reptiles – that
asteroid was a big mistake!"

Michael stood up, concluding, "Anyway, now you know the scale of
the problem. Most of humanity's suffering is self-inflicted, but your
very existence now threatens to destroy *all* life on the planet. Over
seven billion people! I wouldn't be surprised if such overcrowding
contravenes the original tenancy agreement."

Feeling surreal, I was unable to resist making reference to one of my
pet themes, replying, "I share your concern, but it's an uphill task
trying to peddle population control to certain groups – especially to a
couple of major religions I can think of!"

Michael spoke sombrely. "That's a matter touching on free will.
You'll have to refer it to Policy & Planning – I'm from Environment
& Accommodation. However, you must be advised: if this situation
continues without immediate improvement, your next visitor might
well be from Security & Transportation—"

"What – who are they?"

Ignoring my interruption he unfurled his wings, continuing, "—especially if, with regret, we're driven to the final option."

"Which is?"

"*Eviction!*"

With that, Michael vanished. Left alone in the troubled darkness I soon drifted off into an exhausted sleep. Come to think of it, was his last word "*eviction*" or "*extinction*"? Still, it doesn't really matter which word he used because it was only a dream... wasn't it?

# *Serial Killer*

### BRIAN HUMPHREYS

Bianca entered the room, flopped into a chair, and suspiciously eyed the grey open folder on the table.

'We meet again,' said the counsellor. 'You've got quite a history for one so young.'

'I know it looks proper bad,' said Bianca, chewing her grubby nails. 'I know I've killed three times already, but it weren't my fault.'

*It never is,* the counsellor thought, before saying aloud, 'So, tell me about the first one.'

'The first time I killed, I was only fourteen an' strugglin' wiv school and bullyin'. I was a victim.'

'We all get bullied at school. It's a rite of passage thing, like acne and period pains.'

Bianca fidgeted in her seat. 'Whatevva!'

'So tell me about number two.'

'I was fifteen an' should 'ave known betta, an' Dwayne should 'ave known betta, him bein' older than me an' all, but he pushed me an' pushed me an' forced me to do it. We all do stupid fings, right? 'Course, I regret it now. Being a killer ain't good for your CV, not that I want a bleedin' job. I was just saying...' Bianca inspected her finger tattoos of *L-O-V-E* and *H-A-T-E* before setting her teeth to work on the nails of the fingers of her right hand. Her left hand rested on her lap, fresh scars visible on the inside of her wrist.

'Tell me about number three.'

'Check this out, right: I 'adn't killed for yonks...'

'Yonks?'

'About two years, but I started hangin' wiv a rough crowd. They was proper bad, always drinkin' and shootin' up. I still don't know how it happened. Heroin messed wiv me brain an' I was totally messed up, you get me? You eva tried it?'

The counsellor shook her head.

'I don't like killing, 'course I don't,' explained Bianca, 'but I wasn't finkin' right. I 'ad no choice.'

'You had several choices...'

Bianca leaned forward aggressively and growled. 'Listen, mate...'

'I'm not your mate,' snapped the counsellor, leaning backwards to keep space between them.

Bianca regained control and eased back into her seat. 'I don't need no psychoanalysis bullshit. These are the facts, right? I'm off drugs an' I know me 'uman rights. I'm old enough to consent, I'm not ready to 'ave a baby, and I'm under twenty-four weeks. So can I 'ave me fourth abortion, or what?'

# The Peri and Paradise

## VICTORIA HELEN TURNER

Once, long ago, before the dawn of time in the land which was to become Persia, there lived a Peri who was called Fazia. A Peri is an oriental nymph, a kind of fairy, who though usually doing good, by helping mortals, is normally, because of their part in the fall of certain angels, barred from paradise. They can, however, redeem themselves, either by extremely good deeds, or being willing to die for love of a human being, in which case they have the privilege of entering eternal bliss.

The Peri Fazia, however, had neither done good deeds nor been prepared to die for love of a mortal during her allotted two thousand years of life. The life of a Peri is not life in the sense in which humans understand it. Though they may eat, drink, marry, have children like humans, they do not age, and a Peri's body is not the same as that of a human; it is an illusion, somewhere between body and spirit. When their time has come, they are judged, and if they have been evil, then their punishment is total destruction of their personality.

Fazia had swept the earth on wings finer than gossamer during her two thousand years, with no thought for the morrow, let alone the end of it all. She had done no good for herself or anyone else, either of her own kind or mortals. Mortals, particularly men, she had teased and tormented with her almond-shaped dark eyes and long hair, black as night, and her graceful body. In the end, her tormenting had come home to roost!

During her wanderings she had come to a city where the palace was made entirely of gold. It appeared that the young King Amalek, though handsome with everything in the world he wanted, had a heart as cold as ice; he cared nothing for his beautiful wife, Isis. Fazia flew on swift wings through the wide windows of the palace. On seeing King Amalek, she at last fell in love!

She had an idea. His wife was away visiting her parents; she would take on the likeness of his wife to make the king fall in love with her. This she did, but the king did not respond, even though he thought Isis seemed different from usual.

One day the real Isis returned. Amalek had fallen sick; she nursed him, and though he nearly died, her care saved him, and, opening his eyes, he fell in love with the real Isis. Fazia, heartbroken and mad with desire for revenge, conjured up an army of strange soldiers who ravaged the city and murdered the king and his new-found love! Worse – it was the very day that Fazia's life on earth was finished. She drifted up and up through a blue haze until she came to a great crystal gate. The Angel of Death was waiting for her.

"You do not belong here," he said, and, holding up a hand, he showed her a vision of the murdered king and his wife, now embracing paradise.

Remorse came over her. "Forgive me, forgive me." She wept, and felt tears for the first time, for nymphs cannot cry on earth.

The angel, in spite of his dreaded task, was moved by her sorrow. "You know the punishment for your wicked deed – eternal death – but because you know that you have done wrong and you are repentant, there may yet be hope, but your repentance is not enough. You may yet be forgiven if you bring to this crystal gate the gift that is most dear to heaven," and with that, he flung her back down to earth.

The Peri swept the kingdoms of the earth on gossamer wings until at last she found a hero dying for liberty after a battle. Quickly, before he breathed his last, she took the last drop of his heart's blood that he had shed for freedom and she rose up and up until she reached the crystal gate. But the angel shook his head, precious though this gift was; this was still not good enough.

Sorrowfully she returned to earth and eventually she saw a dying lover over whom his beloved wept. The Peri caught up the farewell sigh as his soul departed, and in great hope, she rose once more to the

Eternal Gate. Once more the angel shook his head. This too was a precious gift but was still not that which heaven desired.

Again, Fazia returned to the earth and flew on and on until at last she came to a miserable village where she found a wretched criminal whose life was stained with the blood of wicked deeds, awaiting his awful punishment, but the man was weeping tears of bitter penitence. The Peri, with great joy, caught up one of his tears as it fell and rose up with it to heaven. This time, the angel smiled and accepted the gift, for no gift is as precious to heaven as contrite tears. The crystal gates flew open, admitting the suffering Peri to the arms of paradise!

# Wee, Wee, Wee – All the Way Home

## LYNDA HOTCHKISS

Today was her wedding day. An extravagant confection of silk, lace, pearls and crystals was hidden from view in a pale blue protective cover in the wardrobe of the master bedroom. She hadn't looked at it for several weeks. The wedding dress was the only thing in the wardrobe of the master bedroom; in fact it was the only thing she was leaving in the apartment.

Six months ago, Judith Bacon was organising her stylish wedding to up-and-coming attorney Jack Harper. She was also starting to be noticed as an effective and ruthless divorce attorney in her own right, and everyone thought this was a marriage made in heaven. They had been almost inseparable despite both coping with busy work schedules. That was until Jack started to work extra hours on a couple of difficult but high-profile cases. He had called Judith to say he was working late at the office one particular night because some sensitive papers had just been received by courier, and they could not leave the security of his office. Judith was disappointed but she knew being a criminal lawyer was hard work.

It was an hour or so later that she walked into his law firm's offices with a Chinese meal and bottle of wine. She wanted to surprise him as it was the anniversary of their first kiss, but it was she who got the surprise. The lights in the boardroom were blazing away but the blinds were half-closed. She opened the door slowly, expecting to see Jack head-down over a sea of case papers. Instead she had a waft of Prada perfume, and a view of Jack's little white bottom, his trousers down round his ankles. He hadn't heard her, nor had the recipient of his current enthusiasm, but Judith recognised the Christian Louboutin shoes. It was Amanda Pettifer-Wolf, Jack's boss and one of the senior partners. Judith backed out of the room, and left the meal and wine outside the door. She walked off feeling stunned. She never saw Jack again.

A week later, she plucked up the courage to phone him at his office, but he wouldn't take her calls. Two weeks after that, Judith received notice of termination of tenancy of the apartment they shared. One thing Jack had failed to mention when they had moved into what Judith thought would be their marital home was that it was owned by the company, and since he no longer resided there, she had to vacate the premises within the month. Instead of a rosy future, both professionally and emotionally, Judith was facing being homeless.

Using her adversarial skills, she had taken the matter to court, and had been given six months to find somewhere else to live. That time period would expire in the next few days.

The extension had not helped her come to terms with the broken engagement. She had had to take time off from work, and then she had just stopped going into the office. Her contract had been terminated and her health had started to decline. She ordered take-outs instead of shopping, and wrapped herself in a blanket to watch mindless TV all day, every day. She didn't want to speak to anyone, or see anyone. She had become a recluse.

Now she was packed and ready to leave, especially after local news had reported New York socialite Amanda's engagement to rising star Jack. What should have been Jack and Judith's wedding day was now Jack and Amanda's engagement bash. Even the mayor had been invited.

Standing in the doorway, Judith glanced down to the diamond ring on her finger. She eased it off and reached to place it on the hall table but changed her mind. She tucked it in her purse, grabbed the keys to her beloved BMW and left.

Unable to face looking for somewhere to live, she stood outside the door and decided the only place she could go was to see Taddy. He would help her sort out her life.

Thaddeus Bacon – known as Taddy to his family – glanced nervously at the clock. Another fifteen minutes and they would be here. He only had to wait for the knock, open the door and then go for a meal.

He couldn't settle. He fiddled with wrenches, then went to the restroom. As he wandered back he heard *tap-tap-tap* on the door. They were early!

"Who is it?" he whispered hoarsely behind the door.

"Taddy?" came the reply. "Is that you? It's me, Judith."

"Judith?" said Taddy in amazement. "What do you want?"

"To be let in would be a start!" came the brusque answer.

Taddy opened the door and pulled her inside.

"I see this place is still a mess," said Judith with a sneer. "When was it last sorted out?"

Taddy rubbed his nose before replying. "Must be... ooh, about three or four..." His voice trailed off.

"Was that days? Or weeks?" asked Judith.

Taddy glanced again at the clock. "Years," he muttered.

"Years?" said Judith with shock.

Before the conversation could continue, there was a knock at the door. Taddy started to panic. They mustn't find her here! He looked about and then gave his sister a push.

"Quick!" he said as forcefully as he could. "Down there!"

He pushed her towards an old green Ford with its hood and all its doors open.

"Where? What?" Judith was confused.

Taddy grabbed her more forcefully and pulled her until her face was close to his.

"Get down there in the pit," he rasped. "If they see you, or even suspect you are here, they'll kill you."

Judith did as she was told. There was something in his voice that compelled her to comply without question. Once in the pit, she crouched down to make herself as small as possible while Taddy lumbered to open the shutters. Two sports cars swerved in and switched off their engines. She could hear voices but not what they were saying. Then Taddy started to groan.

"OK, OK!" he was shouting. "Just give me five minutes, just five minutes, please. I need to get something from the office."

"You're supposed to be ready to go!" came another voice, one that made Judith shiver. "Just this once, otherwise the Wolfmen will have to find somewhere else to do business."

"I know. Come with me if you want," said Taddy, making his way up the stairs. "You can watch my every move."

By the way he stressed the "my" in his last statement, Judith knew that was her cue to get out. She waited until the office door closed and then crept out and back to her car.

Ten minutes passed before Taddy appeared. She flashed her lights and he ambled over to her.

"What the hell was all that about?" she remonstrated as he climbed into the passenger seat.

"Don't ask," came the sullen reply. "Better you don't know."

Judith could tell by his attitude that the matter was closed.

"What now?" she said, switching on the engine.

"Drive," Taddy muttered. "Down the block to Taco Bell."

Judith complied, as she had always done where big brother Taddy was concerned.

Judith moved in with Taddy. The neighbours raised a few eyebrows to begin with until she told them he was her brother. They left them alone after that.

After a couple of months, Judith was still there, keeping house for Taddy. The house was a mess, and Judith spent most of her days trying to bring order to the chaos left behind when Taddy's wife had left him, taking their two children with her. She cooked his meals and while they ate, Taddy revealed who the Wolfmen were.

"So this thousand bucks just appears in an envelope on your desk with a date and time and the logo of the Wolfmen?"

"Thass right!"

"You open your garage to them and leave them to it?"

"Thass right."

"Next morning they've gone and another five thou is sitting on your desk."

"Thass right."

"And this happens about once a month?"

"Thass right, 'bout once a month."

Conversation was not Taddy's strong point.

"And when are they coming again?"

"Ah, well, that's the problem," said Taddy, rubbing his chin. "They want to come on Friday."

"Why is Friday a problem?" asked Judith with a slight frown.

There was a brief hesitation. "They want your car as well."

"My car? My car!" Her voice was starting to turn into a shriek. "Why do they want my car?"

There was another hesitation that turned into a pause before Taddy summoned the courage to tell her that the Wolfmen thought he was dealing in cars on the side and against them. They had seen him in Judith's car when he had been heading to the store, and now they wanted it – for a client.

"No way, Jose!" Judith blurted with great indignation. "Do you know how hard I worked to get that car? How many hours doing pro bono work to get noticed?"

"Nope!" came Taddy's response. "Ain't seen you for four years, not since you went to New York. Just the occasional card at Christmas. You turned up on my doorstep looking a might lot bigger than before. Being successful obviously meant eating a lot of pies, eh?"

Judith would have felt guilty about not making more regular contact with her favourite brother, and she felt disgruntled about his remarks concerning her weight gain, but the idea of losing her beautiful BMW had a higher priority at the moment. "Well, let's say it was a lot of sheer hard graft, and that car got me here when everything else was taken from me!"

Judith relived those last few minutes in the apartment, and remembered the diamond ring. Jack had never asked for it back, and she hadn't asked if he wanted it. It was her nest egg now.

"If I don't give it to them, they will take it from me. I mean, you."

"Over my dead body!" spat Judith, her face going red.

"Exactly" was all that Taddy could say.

Judith opened her mouth like a fish, and Taddy nodded. He pointed at her chest with his index finger, the rest of his hand making a gun shape. He mouthed "Bang!" and repeated it, aiming at her head. Her hand flew to her throat.

"We've got to leave!" she said.

"Leave? And go where?"

"How much money can you lay your hands on? We'll need bank cards, cheque books too! In fact anything easy to carry and worth something." Judith was already throwing her personal belongings into a bag, and grabbing some supplies from the cupboards.

Taddy asked the question again. "Where do you think we can go? These guys have contacts everywhere!"

"Not quite everywhere, big brother. We can go home to Paw!"

"Louisiana?" mused Taddy. "Yup. We could lose them there!"

The next day, Judith and Taddy were on their way back home.

From his seat on the porch, Jedidiah Bacon could see a cloud of dust on the horizon.

"Someone's coming," he said, one hand fussing his dog's head. "Too big to be them wolves. 'Sides, just got rid of another, so they won't be back for a while." He spat on the dirt.

There was a shovel at his feet. He picked it up and wiped the fresh dirt off the pan with his hand. He glanced towards a small rise where five small mounds were just visible, two accompanied with crosses. "I'll deal with this, Paw. You rest easy with Mam, 'n' look after little Micah. He's been so lonely for such a long time!"

Jed spared a thought for the little brother he barely remembered, carried off as a toddler with scarlet fever when he was about five or six years old. Mam had chosen where Micah would be buried, and Paw had buried her next to him. Paw had joined them recently but the freshest additions were only a few months old. In fact one was so fresh, the soil was still on the shovel.

"C'mon, old gal!"

Jed got up from the rocking chair, and his faithful hound followed him inside the house.

It was twenty minutes later when a very dusty BMW screeched to a halt outside. Jed watched from behind the net curtains that his mother had saved for a year to buy. A large woman got out and stared at his house. Her passenger eased his bulky frame out of the car and leaned backwards, rubbing his lower spine.

"Looks the same as ever," said Judith, looking at the clapboarding that still needed painting.

Taddy nodded.

"That window was broke when you threw a stone at me when I was fifteen," said Judith, pointing at the offending item. "Why hasn't Jed mended it? Or Paw?"

Taddy shrugged.

"And where are they? We could be anybody. We could have come to rob the place."

Taddy examined his fingernails and muttered, "Not much here worth taking. Never was. One puff of wind and the whole house would fall apart."

Judith was starting to whine. She stepped onto the porch and up to the door. It suddenly opened and a shotgun was poked through.

"What you want?" was grunted.

The shotgun moved a bit further towards her.

"C'mon, speak up. What you want?"

Judith looked at Taddy. He just shrugged and leaned against her car.

"My family used to live here," she said.

"No, they didn't," came the reply. "My family has lived here for the last hundred or so years, so 'op it!"

"So has mine!" said Judith with a touch of indignation, tinged with a little puzzlement. "Gideon? Is that you?"

The shotgun wavered and then was lowered. The door opened slowly, creaking on its hinges.

"Jed! It's you!" she said with a broad smile. "You're looking good. How's Paw?"

Jed frowned. Who were these people? "Paw was took last winter. He's with Mam up the hill."

Realising Jed had no idea who she was, Judith pointed to Taddy. "Look, it's Taddy. And I'm your sister, Judith."

Jed scrutinised both of them, and slowly realisation dawned. Taddy made the effort to stare at the family burial plot.

"Taddy, is that really you?"

Taddy nodded.

"You've grown a bit, and put on some pounds in the process."

Taddy gave an embarrassed smile. "So have you, Jed, so have you."

"So has she," said Jed, using his thumb to indicate his sister. "Quite a few pounds, I'd say!"

Judith bristled and brushed herself down. She had put on some weight since the debacle about Jack, but it wasn't polite to talk about it. "Are we going inside, or are we expected to stay out here?"

Jed blocked their way. "Didn't know you was coming," he drawled. "Place's a bit of a mess."

He lumbered inside, followed by Judith, then the dog, and Taddy reluctantly brought up the rear. Inside it was dark, and dusty, and cluttered with all types of debris and junk. Dirty dishes littered the table, and were beginning to pile up in the sink.

It took Judith several weeks to sort it all out and make it habitable for the three of them. One evening, they were sitting on the porch, drinking home-made hooch, when Judith asked about Gideon. She had tried to ask before, several times, but Jed always changed the subject. Tonight, he had imbibed enough alcohol to loosen his tongue.

"Gideon? He was here just before you came."

"Where's he gone? We could go and visit him," slurred Judith.

Jed thought for a minute. "Not really sure if that's possible. Gideon's not the same any more. He's gone away."

There was a silence between them, broken only by a loud belch from Taddy.

His uninvited visitors were starting to get on his nerves. It wasn't too bad having someone sort out the house, even cook the meals, but neither had offered anything towards their keep yet.

"More wolves," Jed would mutter as he plodded round the homestead finding little things to keep himself busy.

It was about this time that Taddy started spending time out of the house too. Initially he just wanted to get away from his sister's bossiness, but then he found Jed's old red pick-up truck. He was naturally drawn to check it out, and spent several days tinkering under the hood till eventually it spluttered into life. Jedidiah did not seem enthusiastic to have transport again, but he made sure the keys were always in his pocket from then on.

Taddy relaxed for a couple of weeks but then started to get bored again. That was when he found the sedan in an outhouse, a dark blue sedan under an old tarpaulin – just like the one his brother Gideon had owned. He raised the point over dinner that evening.

"Found a car in your barn, Jed."

Jed just nodded, but any astute observer would have noticed the narrowing of his eyes.

"Is it OK if I take a look at it?"

Jed leaned back in his chair and stared at Taddy. "What for? Pick-up's working."

Taddy shrugged. "Give me something to do, I s'pose."

"You could go home," suggested Jed.

Judith ignored the comment and encouraged Taddy to keep busy. A little later Taddy spoke again.

"Our Gideon used to have a car like that."

Jed was sitting on the old sofa and his eyes glittered. He wondered why Taddy was so interested in the sedan. He grunted.

"Why's Gideon's car in our barn?" queried Judith as she shovelled more apple pie onto her plate.

Jed squirmed before answering, "He left it here."

"Strange thing to do," Judith said. "Thought our Gid and his car were joined at the behind."

She chuckled at what she thought was a little joke. Taddy stared out the window at the crosses on the hill. Jed wondered what he could say, deciding eventually to just get up and walk outside. His dog followed him.

"If Gideon came to visit," Judith mused, "how did he manage to leave here?"

Taddy heard her but made no comment.

"Jed could have taken him to the bus route or train and then driven the car back here, but surely Gid would have come back for it as soon as," she went on.

Taddy just shrugged.

"It's got two flats," he put in. "And the pick-up probably ain't moved for a year or more."

Out on the porch, Jed was feeling unsettled. He liked his own company – and that of his dog – more than other humans.

"You know where you are with a dog," he said to no one in particular. "Everyone else is just wolves."

It had been more than six months since his brother and sister had come to visit – and they were still here. She had made everywhere tidy and clean, and made him change his clothes once a week. Baths were regularised to Saturday evenings, and church on Sunday. Taddy had got the old pick-up working, and made the sedan roadworthy once more. He had even commented that it could be worth a few dollars as it was a rare model in these parts.

Jed just wondered when they were going to leave. Wolves were not welcome here.

As the evenings started to get a little cooler, the wolves remained. They needed to be dealt with as soon as he could manage. Jed took up his usual place on the porch, shotgun across his lap and faithful dog by his side.

"You know they're ready to finish us off, don't you, old girl?" he said as he stroked the dog's back. "Soon, they'll be immoveable, and it has to be dealt with in the only way I know."

He caressed the shotgun.

"Soon, old girl, soon it will be just us."

The plans to celebrate Christmas were never completed. The wolves were here, and the Bacon family's shabby little home was rocked to the core.

Jedidiah Bacon sat on the porch, shotgun by his side, and stared at the small family plot where now seven mounds could be clearly seen. He had cleaned the shovel and placed it on the floor in the kitchen, where it used to be before his solitude had been interrupted. His dog ambled up to him and lay down at his feet. Jed knew there were a few thousand dollars in a tin in his sock drawer – courtesy of Gideon's car.

"Taddy was right about the car, old girl, and there's always the Beamer if we need it," he said.

He stared at the diamond ring that glinted in the palm of his dirty work-hardened hand. It was insurance, a little something for the future, his personal nest egg. He felt content, at peace with himself now he was alone again. He stared up at the family burial site, wondering who would put him there when his time came. Would they question who was in the four unmarked plots next to Aaron and Agnes Bacon, and close to little Micah? Did he care? Not really! He was used to his own company, preferred it actually, and now it had returned.

"You know they're finally gone for good, don't you, old girl? It's back to just you and me. No more wolves now."

# *Tartarus*

## GUY JENKINSON

The Black Tarn holds its secret well;
Satan knows, but He'll ne'er tell.
Peer into these waters
And see the vision, clear, below,
Of... the Pit. Mortal, dost thou know
Where He has brought us?
Let's pass beneath this evil pool:
Explore the land where demons drool
O'er their victims' end.
Not a blade of grass, not a fern
Dares trespass in this Devil's Urn,
Where the heavens rend
The evil, clinging, sulphurous mist:
A deadly, creeping, vampire's kiss
Covering the bones
Of mortals, in this world decaying,
For their previous sins now paying
With their anguished moans.
Stern basalt, lashed by stinging sleet,
Cowers 'neath the tempest's beat
Which echoes thro' the night.
The dark veil'd moon and violet sky
Above the pines, where spirits sigh
Out of mortal sight,
And glowing mountains weave a spell
– A rugged ring enclosing... Hell!

*G P Jenkinson – Upper VI^th, Autumn Term 1961.*
*Entry for the Tennyson Poetry Competition (3^rd)*
*King Edward VI^th Grammar School, Louth, Lincs.*

# My Brushes with Royalty

### JENNY MURPHY

## Princess Anne

In 2012, the Princess Royal Trust and Crossroads Care amalgamated to create the Carers Trust. To celebrate I was tasked with identifying carers who would travel, with me, to Butlins in Minehead to meet Princess Anne and to share their carer stories. I chose my group carefully so that their situations had very different caring challenges.

Carers arrived from all over the country and groups were placed in strategic positions around the complex. For my sins, I was allocated spaces adjacent to a circus skills workshop. I was given a summary of the protocol, which should be adhered to at all times. In brief, one should address Princess Anne as Her Royal Highness in the first instance and if conversation permitted in the second instance, it would be permissible to call her ma'am, rhyming with pam. No-go areas were touching her or addressing her as ma, rhyming with pa.

This vital information having been imparted to my excited group, we waited for almost an hour before a murmur went through the waiting participants as she came into view and stopped several yards away from me. I took this short respite to whisper final reminders. Protocol and carers' roles.

At last, she stopped to talk to us.

Sylvia grasped her hand tightly and spoke enthusiastically of her years as a cycling member of the Tufty Club.

Malcolm remembered the Tufty Club exploits and proclaimed that he now intensely disliked meeting cyclists on a hill.

Newly released from Sylvia's grasp, Princess Anne declared that 'one should never overtake a tractor even if one has a four-by-four'.

As for Harold, he stared at her for a moment, collected himself and said, 'Ahhhhh,' and then, more confidently, 'Baaaaa.'

At this, she moved swiftly on before I had the chance to explain the different, challenging roles of all of the carers in my charge.

## Prince Charles and Camilla

I expect that there are very few people who cannot remember a time when they did something stupid. On this particular occasion, I surpassed myself.

My husband and I had been invited to attend a special ceremony in St Paul's Cathedral to celebrate the end of the 'troubles'. Mike had served in Northern Ireland when the problems had been at their worst. The streets were cordoned off to hold back crowds anxious to be part of history. There was a real sense of tradition mixed with pride.

We arrived at the appointed place at the appointed hour and stood quietly while we waited for the band to lead the procession into the cathedral. With clapping and cheering from the crowd, we processed into the cathedral. We watched as Prince Charles walked by the end of our row (short legs) with Camilla in his wake (pecking bird-like motion).

The service ended with precise instructions for the *men*. They were to leave by the west door in order to parade through the streets to the allocated reception areas. It took a few moments for me to register that many of the congregation had left and those remaining had a common sense of purpose. Trying to look in possession of my faculties, I took a slow walk to the front doors of the cathedral in the hope of picking up a spare order of service for Auntie Gladys. Once this had been accomplished, I heard the band strike up with a fast march and I drifted towards the noise. Very soon, I was on the steps with the military personnel waving to the crowds.

I soon got bored of this activity and realised that it would not be long before the parade was out of sight. My destination was to be the Guild Hall for a buffet reception but I had no idea where the Guild Hall was.

Desperate situations need desperate measures. I broke through the police cordon while ducking under the barrier, keeping an eye on the tail end of the procession. I calculated a six-yard separation and sauntered down the middle of the road looking purposeful. After a few steps, I was moving my arms in a low-key march, or so I thought. What I did not know was that to the side of the cathedral, previously out of sight, was a podium. This had been erected so that Prince Charles and the heads of the various armed forces could salute the men as they passed. Their faces were a picture as I brought up the rear. To give them their due, all parties maintained a respectful salute despite the fact that I decided to ignore them. My Brownie days are long gone.

I would have loved to be a fly on the interior of the security forces car.

I was first at the buffet, to the surprise of the royal representatives. They were far too polite to ask where I had suddenly appeared from and why I was at least fifteen minutes early. I could not have thought of an explanation, so it was a very good job I was not asked.

# Skeleton in the Cupboard

## VICTORIA HELEN TURNER

We arrived at the old manor house in the early evening; a high autumn wind pressed itself against the front door like an invisible body as we both, with an effort, pushed it shut, against the elements and the outside world. The slamming of the door echoed around the hall. We relaxed in the warmth of the drawing room with a bottle of champagne.

'Come on, Dorothy,' I said, 'with a family and a house as old as yours, you must have a skeleton or two in the cupboard.'

Dorothy stared deeply into her glass of champagne, curving her lips into a secret smile. 'Well – yes, I can honestly say I have *one* skeleton in my cupboard.'

'Tell me all – or is it a terribly dark secret?'

'It was a secret until tonight, but you do have a right to know – especially as you married me this afternoon *and* made a will in my favour recently.'

'Yes, I suppose that does give me a certain advantage. Incidentally, I'd also like to know if you married me for my money.'

She looked at me mischievously. 'Well, perhaps I did, darling, but of course, that wasn't the only reason.' She placed her glass on the table and put her arms around my neck; our lips crashed together in a kiss – on her part – not so much of passion, but a kind of violence. 'There,' she said, drawing back, 'that's the other reason. Oh no, darling,' she said, seeing my look, 'not *love*, you knew my views on that ridiculous emotion when we met, Alan, but what we feel is a very good imitation, convenient to us both.'

'Did you marry your first husband for the same reasons?' I asked, serious now. I knew she didn't love me; it was a much baser emotion that she felt for me. I admired... wanted her; she was attractive and accomplished – and until this very moment, I had thought I loved her – but something about that kiss suddenly repelled me. Perhaps I should bear in mind that in her teens, she had had an affair with someone, perhaps the only one she had really loved, who had treated her so badly that she had been ill for some time – perhaps it had made her hard – but I knew I had to accept what she was prepared to offer.

She answered my question. 'I married Jack purely for his money – his chain of stores kept this house going.' She looked around the drawing room with its Regency furnishings with a kind of hunger. 'This house and all its traditions are the only things worth loving,' she said in a harsh whisper.

She carried on with a kind of fanatical pride in her eyes that I had never noticed before – or which perhaps she had kept hidden.

'I'm the tenth Countess of Denton – that's what matters to me. Jack's money was poured into the constant upkeep of this stately home – my home – the home of my ancestors. The only other thing Jack was useful for was that he gave me my daughter Cassandra – the next Countess of Denton. So you see, Alan, your oil will be very welcome. Let's have no illusions about that, but,' her face relaxing, 'that doesn't mean we can't enjoy ourselves.'

'You must have waited some time to get your hands on his money – as his body was never found.'

'It was worth waiting for – and it wasn't my fault if he got himself killed climbing stupid mountains in the depths of winter.'

'You'd had a row?'

'Yes – so off he went with all his gear; climbing mountains was his way of escaping reality.' A kind of cold contempt flashed across Dorothy's face.

'Well, don't we all try to escape in our own way?'

'I don't; I'm severely practical. Now, what about another drink?'

I nodded and she refilled my glass and then her own.

'You won't have to worry about me climbing mountains,' I said. 'I'm much too lazy.'

'Oh – pity – then you won't have a convenient accident.'

'Well,' I began, responding to her swift change of mood, 'I do like to drive fast cars.'

'So I *do* have a way out? I could have your brakes fixed!'

'You could – but I have a very vigilant and thorough mechanic.'

'Oh yes, Enrico, that dishy Italian ex-racing driver. I'll just have to think of something else, then.'

'Talking of something else, you've yet to tell me about the skeleton in your cupboard.'

Dorothy sipped her drink. 'Yes, why not, Alan? But have a drink first; you haven't touched it.'

I gulped down my second drink and placed my glass on the table.

'Come on, then; my deadly secret is this way.'

We went into the hall where, as was usual in such an old house, suits of armour stood guard around the walls. Glancing up at the minstrels' gallery, I thought for a moment there was a slight movement; no, must have been the drink. We were alone in the house for tonight; the servants had been given a two-day holiday. 'More romantic, darling,' Dorothy had said. I followed her up the great staircase that led off the hall.

At the top, she turned right, along a corridor lined with the usual ancestral portraits – all of them the living, or perhaps I should say, the dead image of Dorothy, and strange, though I hadn't noticed it before, there was a cruel curve to those long-dead mouths. Come to think of it, the same cruel curve sometimes played on Dorothy's lips, as, for instance, when she had been talking about her late husband. I felt a kind of unease as I followed her along the never-ending corridor, and there was a slight spinning sensation in my head – in fact, I seemed to be losing my balance.

'Hurry up, Alan,' came Dorothy's voice from a long way off. She stopped outside a door, opened it, and went into the green bedchamber. As might be expected, the general murkiness of the room showed a four-poster bed with faded bilious-green velvet hangings, with carpet and curtains to match. In fact, the room looked just like I now felt. Dorothy put the light on, and the bilious colour was highlighted in all its sick glory.

'Now, just for you, Alan – my secret, because there isn't much time left.'

I'd begun to feel rather ill. 'What do you mean – not much time...?'

She carried on as if I hadn't spoken. 'It was so simple to dispose of Jack. I drove his car up to Scotland, with his climbing gear, and I parked at his favourite spot. Nobody saw me. I returned by train,' she continued. 'The only problem was the body.'

The horror of what she was saying filtered through to my fogged brain. 'You murdered him!' I gasped.

'Of course, darling, he'd served his purpose,' she said, perching on the sickly green bed, 'and now you've served your purpose. Feeling rather awful, aren't you? Well, it won't be long now; you'll feel much better in, oh, about five minutes, I should say.'

Truth dawned; the she-devil had poisoned me! 'The drink...' I whispered.

'No, Alan, dear, not the drink; much too obvious. Remember that kiss; remember I was born in the tropics? I know a lot about poisons – poisons that don't leave a trace. Just a small dart in the back of your neck when I placed my arms around you; so simple!'

I vaguely remembered what I took to be her long fingernails digging into my neck.

'Give it a few days,' she went on. 'Your car at the bottom of the cliff, your body in the driving seat, you and car burnt to a cinder. Verdict, speeding. So unfortunate.'

'There's Enrico...'

'Of course there's Enrico – he's here right now.'

A man entered the room – *Enrico!*

'Your excellent mechanic will make sure your car goes over the cliff.'

She got up, walked across to the panelled wall and pressed a section of the carving. A panel slid open, revealing a small room.

'Enrico and I are partners in love *and* crime, you see.' She nodded at him. Enrico shoved me violently through the opening. 'There you are, darling, you'll be in good company.'

There was the sound of her laughter as the door slid to behind me. I heard myself screaming, and saw before me, slumped in a corner, the obscene, grisly remains, the grinning skull – of Jack – *the skeleton in the cupboard!*

# FIFTY-WORD STORIES

### BRIAN HUMPHREYS

## Naughty Boy

In a land of inflatable people, the schoolboy, armed with a pin, stood with slumped shoulders and bowed head before an angry headmaster.

'Well, Jones, what are we going to do? You've let your family down, you've let your friends down, but most importantly of all, you've let yourself down.'

## Do You Ever Think About That?

Just for a moment, let us suppose a giraffe needs a drink of coffee. By the time the coffee has travelled up its neck and down to its stomach, the coffee will be stone cold. Do you ever think about that?

Of course not! Because you only think about yourself.

## You're Mine

'I'll protect you from now on,' he whispered to her, 'now that you're mine.' He watched her breasts rise and fall and listened to her shallow breathing as her eyes moved behind closed eyelids as she lay unconscious on the floor. 'You're almost perfect,' he said. 'Shame you bruise easily.'

## Dance Lessons

After watching Pudsey win *Britain's Got Talent* in 2012, I enrolled my greyhound for dance lessons but, after ten weeks, saw no improvement. I took the instructor aside. 'I'm spending a fortune here. Why isn't my dog's dancing improving?'

'I'm sorry,' the instructor replied. 'Your dog's got two left feet.'

# *Jolly Hockey Sticks*

## FAITH MOULIN

We called her Smitch. I'm not sure whether that was a kind of Anglicised juvenile version of Schmidt with undertones of Nazi Germany, or whether we just found the sound appropriately harsh, matching her tone and her style. She certainly wasn't a Miss Smith, softly purring off the tongue.

Smitch was our Games teacher. It wasn't called PE at our school. It was Games, which meant hockey in the winter, netball and tennis in the summer, and gym all year round. Gym meant torture on the wall bars or torment on the vaulting horse followed by a cold, communal shower, all under her hardened steel eyes.

I remember the shame, the shyness, the utter degradation and humiliation in those lessons. I remember her sadistic ways and her cheerless face, her pitiless punishments and her piercing blue eyes.

One day a sharp hoar frost lay thickly on the ground like a clean sheet, picking out the edges of the dandelion leaves and making patterns of them. Our games lesson was early in the morning and the fog was slow to clear. Smitch was dressed in a nice warm tracksuit, gloves, scarf, woolly hat. We were dressed in our navy blue knickers, canvas hockey boots, ordinary school white nylon socks and short-sleeved Aertex blouses. That day, several degrees below freezing, we were allowed to wear our school jumpers. Big deal. Our breath formed clouds which chuffed out of us as we puffed out of the changing room and headed for the hockey pitch.

"Run!" shouted Smitch. Every lesson before the hockey could start we had to run around the perimeter of the whole field. She called this warming up. "Run!" she shouted, but she stood still. The air was thick with moisture and my hair was getting wet. All the normal outdoor sounds were muffled; even the sharp edges of her voice were muted.

*Blow this,* I thought. *She can't see what we're doing.*

When I reached the other side of the field I stopped running and the others behind me also slowed their pace until we were walking in a bunch – a gang of silent resistance. As I reached the part of the field nearest the hedge I sauntered off into the fog. I made my way along the hedge to where I thought there might be a gap. I couldn't see or hear very far. I was just about aware of the crisp footfall of my classmates as they began to pick up speed and run. I didn't suppose I would be missed.

The cruel commandant voice of Smitch boomed terror into my shaky purple legs.

"Where do you think you are going?"

She was advancing on me, hockey stick raised like a cudgel. I tried to push my way through the hedge but it was too thick. The branches had spent decades weaving themselves together, fastening their thorny twigs onto their neighbours' branches. Now it was a wall of barbs and daggers. Smitch was there right beside me and I realised as I looked into her hard spiny face that I had gone too far. Suddenly she smiled.

"Now I've got you," she said quietly. And I knew.

I knew she was going to kill me with the hockey stick and no one would ever know. It would be an Agatha Christie-esque drama. As the fog gave way to weak white sunshine someone would spot my body lying under the hedge. A doctor would be called who would pronounce me dead at the scene. The police would come and interrogate the school, but no one would have seen anything because no one could have seen anything through the fog.

I had to scream. I must scream.

Nothing. I couldn't even scream. My seized throat froze, obeying her silent wish, stifling any hope. I was shivering from head to toe. Smitch's right arm was raised and in it the appropriate weapon: her hockey stick.

I was found later, at break time, when my groans were heard by a first-former. I was so cold, lying there with my bare legs on the icy ground. They helped me inside and I heard Smitch say, "Oh, she must have lost her way in the fog."

I suppose I passed out. I had no head injuries.

I thought I would never get over it. Even decades later I would wake up shouting and screaming. My breath came in short bursts and, although I never ran away in my dream, my chest rose and fell as if I had been sprinting on Sports Day. My breathing was shallow and staccato, just as it was on that frosty hockey pitch. I felt powerless, just as I had forty years ago in the fog. My feet were pinned to the ground by Smitch's piercing blue eyes. I could only try and try and try to scream until eventually I woke myself up. It was always hard to go back to sleep, my chilled skin prickling, my eyes pricked with tears. I would close my eyes and lie back on my pillow as it rose up again – the same jolly hockey stick.

# *About the Authors*

### PETER CORRIN

I am a 60-something, XXL person with a passion for English. I was initially inspired towards poetry by an English master at school at about 11 and went on to have the good fortune to meet, and be further inspired by, visiting poets to my secondary school, including Seamus Heaney.

My love of words and their employment has resulted in my having an unquenchable thirst for reading and a substantial collection of books, much to the chagrin of my wife! I just cannot part with any books and there is a permanent pressure to find space for them all, only slightly offset by also having a Kindle!

My focus on writing has been helped in recent years by taking early retirement and by finding the Wordsmiths of Weston and Theatre Orchard to encourage me to explore the many facets of the craft of writing, from short stories to poetry and haiku.

### BARBARA EVANS

I am retired and I live in Yatton. I write poetry and short stories.

I like to walk and that is how I find the beauty to write about in my poems. I would like to write a novel soon.

I love to take part in workshops about poets and novelists and I really enjoy the company of other writers. I play guitar and sing in a choir, and in an informal band. I am interested in wildlife.

# *About the Authors*

### LYNDA HOTCHKISS

I became interested in short story writing after telling my closest friend that it might help him get through a breakdown. He challenged me to write, and I picked up the gauntlet with stories of varying lengths. Now the characters come and tap me on the shoulder, begging to be immortalised by words on a page. I can never work out how long a story is going to be, I just go where the characters take me! Nothing has got to the publishing stage yet, despite a mutual collaboration on a series of tales about the trials and shortcomings of a middle-aged man being almost complete. One day, one day...

After moving to the South-West to be closer to family on retirement, I joined this local writers' group and was introduced to the world of competitive writing. I still wait for some form of competition success, but continue to scribble whenever the mood takes me!

### BRIAN HUMPHREYS

With the help of insomnia and tablets the strength of horse tranquilisers, my creative muse has not only been released, it lives in my spare bedroom.

The alphabet consists of only 26 letters, but they produce an infinite number of words for a creative writer to play with, if you allow your mind to explore uncharted waters.

The truth is that when I'm letting a story out, I come alive, with the end result sometimes good enough to draw readers and competition judges into the story (as several awards would indicate). I write for fun, not profit, but feel free to download/buy any of my published books. Some people love to read, and it is our responsibility to feed their addiction.

# *About the Authors*

### JENNY MURPHY

As a mother of three, I was fortunate in being able to involve my children in my working life, be it as a befriender of an elderly person with mental health issues, an extra pair of hands in a family with a seriously ill relative, or as a youth worker. It was my responsibility for the local Phab club that taught me about life from the perspective of an individual with physical or learning difficulties.

With a group of friends to help, I started a small charity to provide structure, skills and above all fun for anyone, irrespective of their personal challenges. The floodgates opened and 15 years on there were 70 different activities a week for over 600 people.

My writing is mainly about the fun I have had during my working life and the debt I owe personally to the individuals who are so underestimated and undervalued, but have made a massive difference to me.

### FAITH MOULIN

I have always enjoyed playing with words but it has been a great help in the last couple of years to meet other people with the same passion. Thanks to their support and encouragement, after years of doing the ironing instead of writing, I now make time to write as much as I can. If you meet me you will know me by the creases in my clothes.

# About the Authors

## SALLY ANN NIXON

Since my childhood, writing has been my passion. Fifty-five years ago, I scribbled tales about my dog, my dolls and my friends. Nowadays, I write stories based on my work and the experience of incidents and people in my life.

It is only recently that I have started to write in earnest. Marriage, mortgages and the mayhem of children and various jobs have always been in the way of any sustained creative flow but since my retirement, I have found the time and energy to pick up my pen and write. It was a surprise to find how serious the stories have become. I'd always been considered a frothy, light-hearted comedic sort of writer. Now things tend towards the reflective, the gothic and the downright nasty.

So, the scribbling continues. I am excited at the prospect of discovering what the future will bring.

## VICTORIA HELEN TURNER

I was born in Birmingham and have been writing since I was fourteen. My first success was a series of children's stories on Radio Bristol. Afterwards, I had poetry and several stories published in anthologies and magazines. My first book was published in 2005; it was a book of children's stories. Since then, three other books have been published, all romantic fantasy. My other interests include singing, vintage films, reading, and listening to Mario Lanza. I share my home with a mischievous black cat called Maria.

For more information, visit my website at vhturner.com.

# About the Authors

### GUY JENKINSON

I was born in 1945, attended Louth Grammar School 1955–62, then, after wasting several riotous years at college, joined Lindsey County Surveyor's Department in 1966. After attaining my Civil Engineering HNC, I took a degree in Maths and IT – so most of my professional life involved engineering and computing.

I started writing short stories for relaxation after my premature retirement in 1995. Being used to formal reports and local government memos, it was challenging to return to the compositional English of my 1959 GCE.

For many years, I was encouraged in the pursuit of authorship by a professional colleague (who is also a close friend), with whom I share several joint ventures.

My favoured genres are sci-fi and horror/fantasy but I have written a few contemporary thriller stories.

My creativity was hampered by a long period of ill-health but it has been re-kindled by my joining the Wordsmiths of Weston (WOW) writers' group.

Lightning Source UK Ltd.
Milton Keynes UK
UKOW04f0238150815

256987UK00001B/101/P